"It's kind of mov

"I think it's sweet that you're crying."

"You do? Surgeons don't cry, though. That's what I was told by my father."

Axel touched Betty's cheek, wiping a tear away with his thumb. "I think it shows more humanity when a surgeon cries."

Her heart was pounding like a jackhammer, her pulse thundering in her ears as she stared into his eyes, the aurora dancing above them. It was just the two of them in the cold darkness. Usually that would freak her out, but for some reason in this moment, with his arms around her, she felt safe.

She felt at peace.

She felt like herself.

And before she could react, Axel cupped her face, leaned in and kissed her. Tenderly at first, before it deepened. His mouth on hers, his hand cupping the back of her head as he kissed her with passion she'd never felt before.

It scared her, but thrilled her, too.

"I'm sorry," he said as he broke off the kiss.

"Don't be sorry," she said breathlessly.

Dear Reader,

Thank you for picking up a copy of *NY Doc Under the Northern Lights*.

This book is special to me because it's my 20th Harlequin Medical Romance. I can't believe it's number twenty. This couldn't have been possible without the awesome editors at Harlequin and my readers!

I love the northern lights, everything about them, and I wanted to set my story in another country that gets to experience the aurora.

Axel doesn't believe he deserves love. Not when he survived a tragedy at sea and his brother was lost. All he wants to do is give his brother's child the best life she deserves and save as many lives as he can. He wasn't expecting love. Especially not from a visiting American surgeon!

Betty is trying to escape a coworker who broke her heart. So she accepts her late father's friend's invitation to work in Reykjavík, which is a world away from New York. She's trying to find herself, and the last thing she was expecting to find was romance, especially under the northern lights.

I hope you enjoy Axel and Betty's story.

I love hearing from readers, so please drop by my website, amyruttan.com, or give me a shout on Twitter, @ruttanamy.

With warmest wishes,

Amy Ruttan

NY DOC UNDER
THE NORTHERN LIGHTS

———

AMY RUTTAN

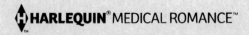

Recycling programs
for this product may
not exist in your area.

ISBN-13: 978-1-335-66379-5

NY Doc Under the Northern Lights

First North American Publication 2018

Copyright © 2018 by Amy Ruttan

Printed in U.S.A.

Visit the Author Profile page
at Harlequin.com for more titles.

This book is dedicated to the people who helped get me to my 20th. My husband, my kids, my parents. I couldn't do this without your faith in me.

Praise for
Amy Ruttan

"From start to finish, this book was entertaining.... The instant chemistry these two have from the moment they're introduced together into the story sets the fast pace of the book."
—*Harlequin Junkie* on *His Pregnant Royal Bride*

"Beautiful, captivating prose and engaging dialogue. The storytelling in *Alejandro's Sexy Secret* is vibrant and unique."
—*Goodreads*

CHAPTER ONE

WHERE IS HE?

Dr. Betty Jacinth's eyes burned. She'd forgotten to take out her contact lenses on the plane when she took the red-eye from Newark to Keflavik Airport, so she was squinting as she pulled her bag through the baggage claim, looking in vain for Dr. Sturlusson, who was supposed to be picking her up.

Dr. Sturlusson was an older physician and friend of her late father, whom he'd met when he'd traveled to Iceland to do a series of lectures before Betty was born. The two had stayed in touch, first through letters, then email, and Betty had only seen her father's friend for the first time on a video call three months ago. When her father died Dr. Sturlusson had sent Betty a card, expressing his condolences and offering her the chance to work for three months in Reykjavik, whenever she wanted.

As her father had done before her.

She had put it off for a long time, but now she was glad to go.

Her ex, Thomas, had married the woman he had cheated on Betty with, and so Betty was definitely overdue for a change of scenery.

Out of sight and out of mind!

She should have left ages ago, but she didn't want Thomas and his newfound bliss to drive her away from her work. The problem was, if she didn't go, then he would always have a hold on her.

Thomas had been her Attending when she was a resident. He'd been there for her when her father died. He'd taught her everything she knew. And she'd thought he'd loved her.

Then she'd found out he'd been seeing someone else. She'd broken it off but Thomas had still been her boss, still overseeing all her surgeries. She'd been stuck in a destructive cycle, her heart broken, her father gone and just paralyzed by self-doubt.

Thomas had used her.

She was a fool.

Yet, as she searched the airport, not understanding a word over the PA system, she wondered if she was an idiot for dropping her work in New York at one of the most prestigious hospitals on the eastern seaboard, to come to Reykjavik.

No. This is good. Then you won't have to face Thomas right after his marriage to Susan.

She glanced at the big windows and saw a vast, flat nothing and that nothing was covered with white. What had she gotten herself into? She wasn't even sure what day it was. Was it Tuesday, yeah it must be Tuesday.

She could always turn around and go back to Manhattan. She closed her eyes and took a deep breath. No, there was no way she could head back. There was no one to go back to. Her father was gone and he'd been her only family. There was nothing left for her there except her job.

A job under Thomas's thumb.

She bit back the tears stinging her eyes. She could do this. She would just have to hire a car and figure out how to drive herself into Reykjavik and the small vacation home she'd rented. Dr. Sturlusson didn't seem the type to leave her high and dry, but perhaps something unavoidable had happened and he hadn't been able to contact her.

She should've told him not to bother picking her up and she should've gone with the car-rental plan in the first place.

Betty glanced up at the signs overhead, try-ing to figure out where to go to rent a car when she saw something move out of the corner of her eye.

She looked over her shoulder and her mouth hung open a little as an over-six-foot Viking of a man came marching toward her. Quickly.

His eyes were trained on her and her knees instinctively weakened, because even from a distance there was an air of command about him. His hair was a dark blond and he had an athletic build. She was pretty sure that he could easily pick her up and toss her a long distance, despite the fact that she was pretty tall herself at five feet nine.

He stopped a few feet from her, those pierc-ing blue eyes settling on her as his gazed briefly raked over her form, assessing her. It sent a shiver down her spine, but not one of fear. His assessment of her was something else, something almost sensual. He didn't smile, his lips pressed together firmly, his strong jaw clenched.

She knew from his posture that he wasn't happy about being here and that got her back up a bit. Why was this stranger staring at her with annoyance? It wasn't as if she were blocking his way, but then again maybe most people made more of an effort to get as far out of his way as possible.

Betty narrowed her eyes and stared back at him, holding her ground.

"Dr. Jacinth?" he asked, almost in disbelief, his voice deep and rumbling.

"Yes. And who might you be?"

"Dr. Sturlusson," he snapped back in annoyance. "I thought that would be obvious."

"No, it's not obvious. I've seen Dr. Sturlusson and he's at least seventy. Are you telling me you're seventy?"

He rolled his eyes. "You mean my father. I am Dr. Axel Sturlusson, his son."

"I see. I thought your father was meant to pick me up."

"He was, but something came up and I've come to collect you." He sounded annoyed by the prospect of taking her into the city.

"Well, if it's too much trouble I can rent a car and drive myself. I wouldn't want to burden you."

"I am here now and you will come with me."

It wasn't 'will you come with me?' It was *you will* come with me and that irked her even more. Dr. Sturlusson was pleasant and polite. His son Axel was a bit of an arrogant jerk.

She should argue with him further, but truth be told she was tired and she was glad to not have to drive.

"Fine," she said. "Lead the way."

He looked down at her shoes. "You do know this is Iceland in winter?"

"I'm aware."

"You're wearing ridiculous heels."

She glanced down at her boots. "They're boots."

"It's icy outside," he stated gruffly.

"Oh, I'm surprised to hear that a place called Iceland is icy," she snapped back. She was too tired to be bandying words about with a gigantic behemoth of a Viking in the middle of the airport.

His eyes narrowed. "I don't appreciate the sarcasm."

"And I don't appreciate your tone, either. I assure you, if I can navigate the likes of Manhattan during rush hour I can get myself to Reykjavik intact."

A small smile flitted at the corner of his mouth and there was a sudden twinkle in his eyes. "Is that so?"

"It is. And I can do all that in heels."

He was openly amused. "Well, my apologies, then, but since I am here already perhaps you'll let me drive you anyways?"

"Thank you."

Axel held out his arm, gesturing in the direction to the terminal doors, and she followed him, pulling her suitcase behind her. She was very aware of the sound of her heels against the airport floor, but she wasn't going to back down to Axel Sturlusson. She hadn't got where she was as a surgeon by backing down. She'd learned how to stand her ground.

Except when it came to Thomas. She'd let Thomas walk all over her and she hated herself for that.

They stepped outside and she was met with a blast of cold, icy air completely foreign to the temperatures she was used to in Manhattan and back home in Tennessee. Her teeth chattered.

Axel turned. "You stay here and I'll pull the car up."

Betty nodded. She wasn't going to argue as she opened up her carry-on bag and dug out an ugly knitted cap and the matching mitts she'd bought at an outdoor store. Fashion be damned, she was freezing her keister off.

It wasn't long before his SUV pulled up and

he got out. In a couple of strides he was beside her, picking up her suitcase and her carry-on and stowing them in the back.

Betty took a step toward the car, but her ankle twisted and she lost her balance.

Before she could hit the cold, unforgiving ground, two strong arms came around her, holding her gently. She looked up into Axel's startling blue eyes. She'd thought they were darker, but up close she could see how deep a blue they were.

And her heart skipped a beat. It was as if those eyes had pierced her very soul. It was unsettling how much the intensity of his gaze affected her.

"I told you those were ridiculous boots. I knew that you were going to slip," he grumbled as he set her upright.

"I didn't see the ice," she said, but she still clung to him.

"Well, you're going to kill yourself walking around in those."

Before she had a chance to respond or react Axel bent over and scooped her up, depositing her over his shoulder, as if he were carrying her from a fire. Upside down she had a good view of his butt. Which wasn't a bad thing, just unexpected for a first meeting. Especially in light of the fact that she was going to be work-ing with him at the hospital. It wasn't the best first impression, but it also wasn't the worst.

"Excuse me!" she hollered, but didn't bother struggling because that would just make things worse.

"What?" he asked, moving toward the SUV, his hand firmly planted on her backside.

"Put me down!" she said.

"I will. Once you're out of harm's way." He stated a matter of fact.

"Look, you great big Viking…you can't treat me like this."

He moved her and then set her down in the front seat of his SUV. There was a condescend-ing, smug smile playing on his face.

"Treat you like what? I got you to the vehicle safely. This way you won't be laid up with a broken ankle during your first month of work in Reykjavik. My father would not be happy if I let harm come to you." He motioned for her to slide her legs into the foot well so he could shut the door.

Fuming, Betty begrudgingly did as he asked, her eyes tracking him as he climbed into the driver's side and buckled in. He glanced at her.

"You should buckle up."

"Do you always manhandle people like

that?" she muttered as she reached for her seat belt.

"Only people who don't know how to appropriately dress in icy weather and may be susceptible to a nasty fall."

Betty's anger melted away and she tried to fight the amused smile that was threatening to erupt on her face.

"I have better boots, but they're in my luggage."

"I do hope so. If not, there is a store not far from your rental where you can purchase a good sturdy pair. You're not far from the hospital, but as that part of town is close to the sea, it can get dangerously icy at times," Axel stated calmly as he drove away from the airport and headed toward the city.

"How do you know where I'm staying?" she asked.

"My father helped you find it. And as I said, he gave me the task of making sure that you are settled. He's quite overloaded with some work at the hospital, so I've been the one dealing with it all."

The last few words were said cautiously and she could see his jaw clench under the stress. She almost wondered if Dr. Sturlusson Sr. was sick rather than overworked and if Axel was hiding it. She knew that look well. She knew the pain and the pressure one carried when a parent was dying. Her mother died when she was young and it had just been her and her father for so long. Then he got sick and it was just her caring for him while trying to do her first year as a resident.

"I'm sorry to hear that your father is ill," she said gently.

"Who said he was ill?"

"Your expression. Your tone of voice. I thought—"

"He's a busy man," Axel snapped.

"Okay."

"He doesn't have time for much," Axel muttered darkly. He didn't elaborate. He just kept his eyes on the road, his jaw clenched and those blue eyes dark and serious.

"Sorry for making an assumption. I lost my father some time ago and I know they were about the same age."

"It's all right," he said gently. "And I'm sorry. My father spoke highly of your father."

"Thank you."

Betty turned and gazed out of the window, her eyelids becoming heavy as the exhaustion that had been pestering her finally caught up with her.

* * *

Axel could hear her deep, even breathing and he glanced over at her. Her head was pressed against the window and she was fast asleep. She was quite beautiful. He hadn't been expecting that. He didn't know what he had been expecting, to be honest, but he hadn't been expecting her.

Blonde hair, brown eyes and a pixie-like face. She was tall, or at least taller than the women he was used to dating. Although it was hard to tell because of the heels. She seemed to have a bit of fire in her, but one that she was suppressing and he couldn't help but wonder why.

Axel was attracted to her but, with his past and the fact that Betty would only be in Iceland for a short time, there was no point acting on that attraction.

He relaxed, but only fractionally.

When he had been ordered by his father to take on the role of assisting the new American surgeon in her three-month placement he'd instantly been outraged.

"I don't want to babysit some American surgeon."

"You need to do this, Axel," his father had

said sharply. *"I don't have time to deal with her."*

Axel had been able to feel the pain in his father's eyes even without looking directly at them. He'd become an expert at it since the accident two years ago. He still couldn't look his father in the eye. Not really.

"I'm here to save lives, not babysit another surgeon who outranks me."

"And whose fault is that?"

"I do my work. I save lives!"

"You're not striving for anything better. You're not publishing papers or doing anything innovative. There will be no more discussion about this. You're doing it."

Axel really hadn't been able to say no. His father was the Chief of Surgery and was Axel's boss now that he was no longer part of the tactical coast guard and worked as a surgeon in the hospital. He just wanted to save lives and go home. He didn't want anything more. He didn't deserve anything more.

He'd worked with Americans before and they hadn't been pleasant to him. So when he'd gone to the airport to pick up Dr. Betty Jacinth, he hadn't been expecting the woman he'd found waiting for him.

Her beauty stunned him. Sure, she had a

feisty little temper, but there was a vulnerability beneath her surface and he wondered what had made her that way.

What had hurt her?

What made her feel as if she needed to prove herself in front of him? Prove that she was so strong, when really he could see that her confidence was shaken under the surface.

That he understood.

He could still hear the screams, sme l the smoke and feel the icy cold water cut thr ugh his skin like daggers.

Get control of it.

Axel rolled his shoulders as he banished the thought away. It was hard, especially during the winter months when the thoughts of the helicopter crash crept closer. The botched rescue attempt.

His elder brother drowning beside him.

He was the only one who survived, when he should've been the one who died.

Now, Axel was guardian to his fourteen-year-old niece, Eira, and he had to deal with the fact that his father blamed him for Calder's death. His niece certainly did.

Don't think about it.

Betty stirred in her sleep and Axel glanced

at her only briefly. Working with her was going to be harder than he'd originally thought.

Maybe his father would take pity on him and step in, especially if his father saw how working with her would be a struggle. He wasn't completely sure how he was going to manage that, but he'd find a way. He couldn't work with Betty. Her or anyone.

He was better on his own. Focused on saving lives and taking care of Eira. That was all he could handle in his life and that was all he really deserved.

His PTSD and Eira were baggage that women couldn't handle and he was fine with that. Eira and his work were his priority. Too bad he was also failing at that. Lives he could save, but dealing with a fourteen-year-old girl was something else altogether.

Still, Eira had no one else and he'd promised his brother he would care for her as they'd clung to what was left of the helicopter in the stormy North Sea.

Betty woke with a start, jolting Axel from his musings.

"Are we there?" she asked drowsily.

"Nearly," he said, gently.

"Good." She sat up and stretched. "Sorry I dozed off there."

"Doesn't matter. You're tired and you need to get your sleep. You start in a couple of days and the shift starts at five in the morning. I'll come and pick you up."

"I can walk to the hospital."

"It's still dark at five in the morning. I will pick you up."

"Fine. I guess that's okay. I don't want to get disoriented on my first day."

"You will have obstacles. Language, for one."

"I can speak a bit," she responded in a bit of broken Icelandic. "And I believe most people here speak very good English."

He laughed. "You are right. When did you learn Icelandic?"

"My father spoke Icelandic because he spent a few years working here before I was born. That's how he and your father became friends. My father came here to work and met your father and then they corresponded for years. My father loved it here and taught me a few words of the language.

Axel shrugged. "I never thought to ask how my father knew yours, but I guess it makes sense. My father is not much of a traveler, so I couldn't really picture him going to the US."

Silence fell between them.

He pulled down a side street off the Hverfis-gata that wasn't far from the hospital. Her little rental was a small blue-green cottage that had a view of the water. It made his stomach twist in a knot as he looked out over that cruel, unforgiving stretch of sea.

He used to love that wide expanse of churning blue, now he hated it.

"Here you go. I'll help you in." Axel didn't give her a chance to protest. There would be icy patches down by the sea and it was windy. As soon as he stepped out of the car he could feel salty mist spraying his face.

"Hold on, Calder. Help is coming."

"I... I can't." There was a wound on Calder's face; his eyes were closed. "Promise me."

Axel knew what he was talking about. "I'll look after her. Don't worry, but just hold on."

"I'm so cold."

"You okay?" Betty asked as he opened her door and then he realized he was blocking the way.

"Fine." He reached down to pick her up, but she held up her hands.

"I've got it. Thanks."

Axel didn't fight her and stepped back. He grabbed her luggage from the back and followed her up the path and the few stairs as she punched in a code on the lock box and got the key. His pulse was thundering in his ears, because every fiber in his being was telling him to get away from the water.

Once they were inside, he set her luggage down.

"I'll pick you up Thursday morning at five."

"You don't have to…"

"No, I'll be outside. Waiting." He didn't want to argue with her. He just needed to put some distance between himself and her, the sea, from it all.

"Okay," she said. "I'll see you Thursday, then."

Axel nodded and left. He could hear her shut the door behind him. He should've offered to help her get groceries. Show her around a bit more.

His father had made it clear that she was his responsibility, but then Calder had been his responsibility too and look how that had turned out.

He'd show her the ropes of the surgical floor in Reykjavik, but that was all.

That was all he could give.

CHAPTER TWO

THERE WAS A knocking at Betty's door early the next morning. An incessant pounding that permeated into her dreams and gave her a raging headache. She opened her eyes, rolling over and looking at the clock on the nightstand. It was nine in the morning Icelandic time, which meant that it was four in the morning in New York City.

Good Lord.

Betty rubbed her eyes and heard the pounding again. It startled her.

Who was at her door? She knew no one here, except Axel and his father and it wouldn't be either of them. Would it?

She clambered out of bed, jammed her glasses on her face, threw a sweater over her tank top, pulled on her heavy woolen socks and made her way downstairs, bumping into a wall as her eyes adjusted to the daylight.

She cursed under her breath and then peeked through the peephole and groaned when she saw a familiar six-foot Viking standing on her porch, looking just as good and put together as he had yesterday.

What does he want?

She opened the door a crack. "What?"

Axel's gaze raked her up and down, just as it had when they'd first met. It was unnerving.

"You just open the door to strangers?" he asked, annoyed.

"You drove me home. You're hardly a stranger."

"You don't know me."

She ran her hand through her hair and tried to stifle a yawn. "So, you've come to my place, early in the morning, on my first full day in Iceland to give me a lecture on stranger danger?"

He cocked an eyebrow. "Stranger danger? I don't understand. What are you talking about?"

"It's…" Betty trailed off. Clearly it was a language-barrier thing and she didn't have the patience or brain power to explain the phrase's meaning to him or argue about it with him. "What do you want, Axel?"

"Can I come in?" he asked.

"Sure." She opened the door wider and he slipped inside. She closed the door and crossed her arms, leaning against the doorframe for support.

"You look terrible," he said.

"It's called jet lag and I was sleeping until I was rudely interrupted."

"The only way to beat jet lag is to pretend it's not real."

"Really?"

"Yes, you should've got up a couple hours ago and started your day."

"Look, have you just come to insult me or are you here for a reason?

Axel glanced over his shoulder. "Let's have some coffee."

And before she could argue he was striding into her small kitchen and rifling through her cupboards. What was with this guy?

Betty followed him, still a bit woozy from her lack of sleep. She tripped over a rug in the hall and Axel reached out to steady her, stopping her from doing a face-plant. His strong arms were around her once again and she was completely mortified.

"You're not too nimble on your feet," he said with a hint of humor in his voice.

She pushed out of his arms. "Axel, what're you doing here? I know you didn't just drive all the way over here to make me coffee."

He turned back to the coffeemaker. "I've come to check on you and make sure you know your way around the city. Also to make sure you get food."

She wanted to tell him that she was fine, but she wasn't. She knew a few Icelandic words and phrases thanks to her father's teaching, but last night when she'd been struggling with jet lag she'd tried looking up stores in Reykjavik and couldn't make heads or tails of the names.

"That would be great," she said. "I'll go get dressed."

Axel nodded. "Good. Don't trip going up the stairs."

Betty glared at him and took the stairs slowly, just so he wouldn't keep remarking on her klutzy tendencies. She wasn't such a klutz when it came to the operating room. When she was there she was in her element.

Was she?

She tried not to think about Thomas. About how he had always been in the operating room with her. Always the lead surgeon. At first, she'd loved having him there. It had been re-affirming. Thomas had been her teacher and he'd given her strength.

But since his betrayal his presence had annoyed her and shaken her confidence to the core, which was another reason why she was here. She was determined to prove to herself that she didn't need anyone's assistance when it came to surgery. That she was better than she thought she was.

She got dressed and made herself presentable. By the time she was done brushing her hair she could smell the coffee brewing downstairs.

When she came back down into the kitchen Axel handed her a cup. She took a sip and it was delicious. She couldn't remember the last time anyone had made her coffee. Thomas certainly never had when they were dating.

"This is good," she said. "Thank you."

"You say that in a shocked tone."

"Well, you are a stranger. I don't know how you make coffee. It could be complete doodoo."

He cocked an eyebrow. "Doo-doo?"

"Garbage."

"Ah, well, I suppose so. Are you ready to go?"

Betty finished her coffee and set the mug in the sink. "Yes, let's get this over with."

"I hope you have your better boots today. It's quite icy being this close to the…to the water." There was an edge to his voice as he mentioned the water, as if he hated it. Betty shook that thought off; perhaps he just didn't like ice, and she couldn't blame him. She wasn't a huge fan of it herself.

"Yes. I have better boots." She picked them up off the floor. "See?"

Axel nodded in approval. "Well, let's go and I'll drive you to the nearest store and make sure you get enough food to survive. I don't want my father saying I let you starve."

"I can find my way around."

"Oh?" he asked as she locked her front door. "What street do you live on?"

"I live on Vatn…"

"I thought as much. You live on Vatnsstigur. That's the correct pronunciation."

"Thanks," she said dryly.

They walked down to his SUV and he held open the door for her. She shouldn't be going with him to get groceries, but she did need food and she was tired and didn't know her way around Reykjavik. She would take his help for this and that was it.

No more.

She was here to make it on her own and not rely on someone else.

The drive to the grocery store was silent, but she really didn't know what to say to him.

Everything she said seemed to annoy him and vice versa. Thankfully it wasn't a long ride and soon they were pulling up in front of a grocery store that advertised being open twenty-four hours a day.

"We're here."

"Good," Betty said, stifling another yawn. "I'm going to need more coffee."

"Well, after we get your groceries home I will take you for a proper coffee near your place. That will wake you up."

"If the cold air doesn't wake me up I doubt any coffee will," she muttered.

"You haven't had this coffee yet." He got out of the car and Betty followed him. He walked well ahead of her in big, commanding steps making it hard to keep up with him.

"Hey!" she called out. "Wait up."

Axel paused and turned around. "What? Did you fall?"

"No, I didn't fall. Why are you always assuming I'm falling or tripping?"

"Because you keep doing it," he stated in a matter-of-fact tone. And he had a point. She had been.

"I'm not falling this time. You're just walking too fast. You're a giant and I can't keep up, not in these boots."

There was a twinkle in his blue eyes. "Sorry."

"Thank you."

"I'll get a cart." He grabbed a cart from the carrel. "You ready?"

"I didn't make a list."

"We'll get you what you need."

"Okay." Betty followed him in a daze. He took her through the produce section and she picked out some apples and oranges. Then they moved over to the deli and bakery. Axel dutifully pushed the cart in silence but after a few aisles he made a "hmm" sound.

"What?" she asked as she held a box of pasta.

Axel reached into her cart and pulled out a can. "This is an interesting choice."

"Isn't it tuna?"

"No, it's lutefisk. You know what that is?"

"Not tuna?"

"No, it's an aged stock fish and lye. It's sort of like gelatin."

Betty made a face. "Oh."

Axel chuckled. "You want me to put it back?"

"No, I'm going to try it."

Now it was his turn to make a face. "You're brave. I don't like it much."

Betty took the can and placed it back in the

cart. "I'm going to try it. I'll be brave. I like fish."

Axel looked amused but didn't say anything more. Satisfied that she had enough to last her for her first few days, she paid for her purchases and he helped her load them into the car. Returning to her rental, Axel helped her take the groceries inside and put them away. She was hoping he would leave when they were done, but he lingered.

"What?" she asked.

"Coffee, remember?"

"Oh, I thought you were just being polite."

"No, I mean it. I'll get you some good coffee. It's not a far walk from here."

"Okay. Isn't it a little cold to be walking though?"

"You wanted to walk to the hospital on your first day and that's farther than the coffee house."

"You have a point," she said. "Okay, let's go, but then I have to get back and prepare for tomorrow."

"Deal."

Axel was right, it wasn't far from her rental, but when they got to the coffee house it was packed and there was nowhere to sit, let alone move.

"Sorry about that," Axel said as they left.

"It's okay."

"I promised you coffee for dragging you out."

Betty looked around and down on the pier near the beach was a little coffee hut. "What about there? That looks like a coffee place!"

Axel looked to where she was pointing and his expression hardened. "Uh."

"We can have coffee and go walk on the beach."

"No," Axel snapped. "No, that's not a good place."

"But it's not crowded at all."

"I said no!" Axel's jaw was tightened and he wasn't even looking in the direction of the beach. "You know what, I have to go."

"Oh," she said. "Okay."

"Let's go. I'll walk you home." He took her by the arm and practically dragged her from the beach. Someone really didn't like water and she wondered why.

That's not your concern.

She was out of breath by the time they reached her rental and he wouldn't look her in the eye as he opened the gate into her yard.

"Thanks for taking me out. I'll see you Thursday."

He nodded curtly. "Thursday. Tomorrow."

And before she could say anything else to him, he walked quickly to his SUV and left. Betty was too tired to figure out what had happened and it really wasn't her problem. She was here to work, not make friends, and that was all there was to it.

CHAPTER THREE

BETTY SIPPED HER COFFEE, her body stil. not used to the time-zone change, even after having had a couple of days to adjust. She was glad that she'd got proper coffee befor: her first day of work. No matter what she ried she still couldn't brew as good a cup of c)ffee as Axel had.

Axel.

That had been a good second day. He'd helped her get groceries, made her feel s me-what welcome, even if her suggestion to valk on the beach had gone a bit awry.

She took another sip of the coffee, wishing she could go back to bed so she could feel nore rested for this important day.

It was currently midnight in New York City, usually the time when she'd be thinking about going to bed.

And the bed in the rental was comfortable.

It had a thick, down duvet and two feather pillows.

Stop thinking about bed.

She set down her travel mug and picked up the parka she'd bought, pulling it on and glancing out of the window just in time to see Axel's SUV pull up.

He's punctual.

She didn't know why in this moment that thought surprised her. He didn't strike her as the kind of man who was usually late. Granted, he'd been late picking her up the other day at the airport, but he had been annoyed and grumpy, so being late had probably irked him.

Why are you dissecting this?

She shook her head. Man, she was tired.

Betty grabbed her bag, her travel mug and her keys. She was ready to face the day, meet the elder Dr. Sturlusson and discuss her lecture series for his surgical residents later in the week. Not only was she working in the emergency room as a trauma surgeon, but she'd been hired to teach the first-year surgical residents. She was terrified because she'd never done this before.

You've got this.

Though there was a part of her that wasn't quite sure that she did, indeed, have this.

* * *

"You can't go to Iceland," Thomas had said as he'd followed her from the scrub room.

He hadn't taken the hint that she wanted to be alone. She'd wanted to cry, to weep, because he was getting married to someone else. He had used her.

"I can and I am."

Thomas had stood in front of her. *"Where can I reach you, then?"*

"For what?"

Thomas touched her cheek. *"You're my rock."*

"I'm going," she'd said, her voice shaking.

"You'll come back," he'd snapped. *"You can't possibly handle it."*

She locked her door and headed down the steps toward Axel's SUV. He got out and pulled open the gate for her.

"I've come to check that you're wearing appropriate footwear."

Betty stuck out her leg. "Happy? You saw these the other day."

He looked her up and down, then nodded. "Yes. Quite. I won't have to carry you into the hospital."

Betty ground her teeth. "And I won't have to slug you now."

"Slug me?" he asked, as he shut and latched the gate behind her.

Betty held up her fist, but the effect was lost, buried under a thick, wool mitten.

Axel raised his eyebrows. "Oh, I see."

And then he chuckled as he opened the passenger door.

"Why are you laughing?" she asked as she slid into the warmth of the SUV's interior.

He shut the door and then walked around to the driver's side, still chuckling as he buckled up.

"What is so funny?" she asked again.

"Slugging. I find it humorous that you think you can harm me."

"I'm tougher than I look, partner. Or, I've been told I am."

Truth be told, it had been a long time since anyone had told her that. She used to be a tougher woman and she hated herself for burying that part of her, for letting Thomas bury that part of her.

Let it go.

"I don't doubt it," Axel said, a hint of humor in his voice. She glanced at him and even in the dark of the car she could see a glint of a humorous twinkle in his eye.

She snorted and took a sip of her coffee.

Axel turned around at the end of the dead-end street where her rental was and sped toward the hospital a couple of blocks away. As they drove through the darkened streets, she could see a green hint in the distance, above the city.

"What is that?" she asked.

"What?" Axel asked.

"The green light on the horizon. What is that?" Something was gnawing away at her that she should know.

"It's the Norðurljós, the northern lights. Have you never seen them?"

"No," Betty said, excitedly craning her neck to look at them. "I live in New York City and there are so many lights there. You can barely see the stars. I also grew up in southern Tennessee. Not exactly close to the sixtieth parallel, but they've always been on my bucket list."

She smiled as she watched the green lights just beyond the horizon. They flickered, but just barely and the light was fading.

"It's hard to see them here. They're stronger around midnight and you can see them much more clearly outside the city. They must be really strong tonight for us to see a glimpse of them here."

"I would love to see them properly one

night." The words slipped out of her mouth before she had a chance to stop them.

"Would you? Well, I can drive you to a great spot I know if you want."

Warmth flushed her cheeks. She hadn't meant to fish for a date from him.

"You don't have to."

"Do you have a car?" he asked.

"No."

"Then I'll take you. I don't mind." He parked his SUV. "You are my responsibility."

"I'm not a child. I'm going to rent a car to get around. You took me out to get food. I think your job is done. I've settled in."

"I will drive you."

Betty got out of the SUV and shut the door. "I'm a grown woman, a talented surgeon and I've been taking care of myself for a long time."

"Why are you so defensive?" Axel asked.

"I don't need anyone to help me." She *was* being defensive, but she didn't want help. Iceland was her chance to prove herself.

To whom? Thomas? He doesn't care.

She shook that thought away. No, she wasn't going to let all these self-doubts take over. She wasn't going to let Thomas ruin this.

She would use the distance. She needed to get over him.

To get over the hold he had on her.

"I'm sorry," she said, wincing as she gripped her travel mug. "I'm just used to doing things on my own."

"I get that," he said. "Same with me."

"Good." She stared up at him. He really was the most handsome man she'd ever seen. It was almost classical. As if he were a Viking hero.

Like Beowulf.

And right now, she felt like a complete Grendel.

"Let's go," he said. "Or we'll be late and I don't like being late."

She nodded and followed him into the hospital.

Great way to alienate yourself from your coworkers, Betty.

This was going to be a long, long first day.

Axel glanced up from where he was charting to see Betty bending over a patient with her stethoscope and listening to the patient's chest. Her blonde hair was tied back and the aquamarine of her scrubs suited her.

Look away.

Only he couldn't tear his gaze from her.

She had spirit. Even if that spirit grated on his nerves, Axel couldn't help but admire her for that. The day he'd spent with her had made him forget all the stress he usually bore on his shoulders.

He'd enjoyed the simplicity of buying groceries and sharing a laugh, the adult companionship aspect of it.

That was, until she'd suggested walking along the beach. That was when it had all gone sideways and he was still angry at himself for the way he'd treated her. This was why he didn't get involved with anyone and why he kept to himself.

"She seems to be fitting in well."

Axel tore his gaze from Betty and glanced at his father, who was suddenly standing across from him, looking formidable in his white lab coat and expensive suit. He didn't see eye to eye with his father on many things, including the expensive tastes his father had.

His father had never understood Axel and Calder's need to go to sea. He saw it as them wasting their medical training by serving in the tactical navy. Patrolling the coast of Iceland and providing emergency medical services at sea.

After the accident, his father had taken the

opportunity to point out that if Calder and Axel had listened to him in the first place and pursued "proper" medical positions, Calder wouldn't be dead.

"First Eira's mother dies of cancer when she's an infant and now her father is lost at sea. Now Eira is an orphan. Calder never should have died."

His father's pained words still haunted him and he knew that Eira thought the same things too. He could see it in her eyes when she was mourning Calder. Or when she thought about the mother she never knew.

Axel was all Eira had now. An uncle who knew nothing about raising a teenaged girl.

"Yes," Axel replied. He was hoping that would be the end of the conversation, because, even though it had been two years since Calder died, it was still hard. To know that his father had loved Calder more and wished that Calder had been the one to survive.

I wish that too. It would be easier than bearing this burden.

"Did you give her my apologies about not being able to pick her up at Keflavik?" his father asked.

"I did. I told her that you were busy."

His father was always busy.

"Thank you," his father said stiffly. "I would've gone, but…"

"I know you were too busy, Father. Eira and I both know how busy you are."

It was a dig. His father barely came to see Eira.

His father's eyes narrowed. "I take my work very seriously, which is why I'm Chief of Surgery here."

Axel shut the chart and set it down on the counter of the nursing station where he'd been working. He took a step closer to his father. "I take my work seriously too. I'm saving lives!"

"Except for one." The words his father spoke stung Axel, because he couldn't save Calder and his father could never forgive him for that. His father took a step back and straightened his lab coat. "I should go and make my introductions. She seems to be done with the patient for now."

"Yes. Do that," Axel said, annoyed with his father's stubbornness as he watched him cross the triage area and introduce himself to Betty.

Axel's head pounded and he turned on his heel, walking away.

His father was so stubborn. If his mother were still alive… He let that thought trail off because he knew his mother would never have survived losing Calder, the favored son.

Calder was the favorite, whereas Axel had always been the screw-up.

Calder had been the only one to love and support him when he was growing up and then messing up his life. It was why Axel had wanted to go into the tactical navy. It was why he'd wanted to be a naval surgeon like his brother. His plan had never been to work in a hospital.

Of course, his plan hadn't included losing his brother and almost drowning.

Axel stepped inside an on-call room that was empty and took a couple of deep calming breaths as the post-traumatic stress disorder began to take control of him.

You can control this wave.

The therapist working with him on his PTSD had taught him the deep-breathing technique. He kept his eyes closed and kept breathing in and out, trying to drown out the sounds of the helicopter crashing into the water, of Calder's last words or the howling of the stormy seas.

Instead he saw Betty's face in his mind's eye. That saucy, feisty pixie-like face. It startled him to see her there.

He scrubbed a hand over his head. Angry

that he saw Betty's face in his mind, mixed in with his torment.

He already knew that he had to be careful when it came to dealing with Betty Jacinth. This only reinforced his conviction to keep things strictly professional between them.

His phone buzzed and he frowned when he saw that it was Eira and that Eira was headed to the emergency room.

What in the world?

Axel pocketed his phone and rolled his shoulders, making sure that he had regained his composure before leaving the on-call room.

Axel headed to the emergency room, hoping his father hadn't gotten word that Eira was in the hospital. No doubt Axel would be blamed for whatever had gone wrong.

He was always the one to be blamed.

It was always his fault, because Axel wasn't Calder.

"Where is my niece?" Axel asked the head triage nurse.

"She's in pod four with Dr. Jacinth. Bed three."

"Thank you." Axel headed over to pod four, which contained six beds. Bed three had the curtains drawn and he could see Betty's shoes under the curtain.

He hesitated, then cleared his throat. "Is it okay if I come in?"

Betty peeked through the curtain. "Dr. Sturlusson, can I help you?"

"Your patient is my niece. I'm her guardian."

Betty's eyes widened.

"Is that my uncle?" Eira's sweet voice came from inside the curtained bed in almost perfect English.

"Yes, if Dr. Sturlusson is your uncle," Betty answered Eira.

"Yes. Or it could be my grandfather."

"No, I don't think it's your grandfather," Betty teased as she stepped to the side to let him by.

Eira looked so small against the bed. Her arm was wrapped up and he could see blood on her shirt and seeping through the wrapping.

"What happened?" he asked, instantly feeling guilty that he hadn't been there for her.

He was never going to get the hang of balancing working and being a guardian to a teenage girl.

How had his brother ever managed?

"I slipped in a puddle of water in the bathroom at school."

Axel gently pulled away the gauze and could

see the angry, ragged wound on her arm. It didn't look as if she'd just fallen on the floor. It looked as if she'd hit something metal and sharp.

"I'll help you. It'll be okay."

"Uh, I don't think so," Betty said, stepping in. "You're her family. You can hold her hand, but I'm the doctor here."

Axel wanted to argue with Betty, but she was right in this case and he didn't want to upset Eira.

Axel stepped away and then took a seat on the opposite side of the bed.

Eira looked uncomfortable. As if she didn't want him to be here.

"Uncle, if it's all the same to you I would like to talk to Dr. Jacinth, privately." A pink blush crept up her cheeks and Eira couldn't even look him in the eye.

"Okay. I will just be outside the pod doing some charting. If you need me I can be back here right away."

Eira nodded and he left.

Betty closed the curtain and his stomach sank.

Eira and he used to be close, back when he was fun Uncle Axel and not her parental figure.

Just another way his life had changed since the accident.

He missed the way it used to be.

Betty could tell that Axel was sad that he was asked to leave but she could tell that Eira was uncomfortable. She couldn't help but wonder what had happened to the girl's parents. Axel hadn't even mentioned that he had a niece, but then again Axel wasn't terribly forthcoming about anything except for the fact he disapproved of her winter footwear and didn't think that she was capable of walking anywhere safely.

"So, what did you need to speak to me about? Or was that just a ruse to get rid of your uncle?" she asked as she pulled a chair over and began to gently clean the wound.

Eira winced. "Well, a bit of both, I suppose."

"Well, you can talk to me. There is a doctor-patient confidentiality that I can't violate."

Eira sighed. "I didn't slip. I fainted."

"Fainted?"

Eira nodded. "I started…there was…blood." A blush crept up the girl's neck and bloomed in her cheeks. Betty completely understood.

"How old are you, Eira?"

"Fourteen, but I will be fifteen soon. I know it's late for... I'm the last of my friends to get it."

"It's not late. If you were over sixteen and hadn't had the onset of menarche I'd be worried then. I was fourteen too when it happened for me."

"You were?" Eira seemed relieved. "My mom died when I was little so there's no one to talk to about these things."

"I get it. Your uncle or your grandfather aren't exactly people you feel comfortable talking with about it."

"Right." Eira blushed.

"I understand completely."

"You do?"

Betty nodded as she continued her work on Eira's arm, cleaning the wound. When she'd fainted, Eira had cut her arm on a metal grate, so it needed a few stitches. A resident or an ER doctor could handle this, but it was slow and they weren't busy. Betty didn't mind.

"My mother died when I was a baby and it was just my father and me. He was a surgeon too, but... I had a hard time talking about it with him. Thankfully my grandmother in Tennessee was still alive and she guided me through my first monthly."

Eira frowned. "My grandmother died before I was born and my mother died shortly after my birth. I just had my dad but..." Tears welled up in Eira's eyes and she wiped them away with her good sleeve. "He drowned."

"I'm sorry to hear that," Betty said gently. "Was it recently?"

"Two years ago. My uncle Axel was my guardian and I went to live with him after he recovered."

"Recovered?"

"My uncle Axel was in the same accident as my father. They were both doctors in the tactical navy. They were in a helicopter on a training mission over stormy seas when there was an engine failure. The helicopter crashed. Everyone but my uncle died."

Betty's heart sank. It explained so much. The aloofness. The aversion to water. That must be a hard thing to overcome.

It made her issues seem silly.

"I'm sorry to hear that," Betty said. "How about I get you cleaned up so you can get out of here? Do you want me to talk to your uncle? Explain what happened?"

Eira nodded, a relieved expression on her face. "That would be great, Dr. Jacinth."

Betty smiled. "You can call me Betty and,

I don't mean to overstep, but if you have any other questions I'm here in Reykjavik for the next three months and I would be happy to help you any way that I can. Your grandfather and my father were friends so it's the least I could do."

"I would like that."

"Good. Now, sit tight and I will be right back."

Betty collected up the soiled gauze and disposed of them. As she went to get Eira some sanitary napkins, she found Axel pacing outside the pod, not charting as he'd said he was going to do.

And she couldn't blame him.

"How is she?" Axel asked.

"She'll be fine. I haven't done the sutures yet. She wanted me to talk to you about something delicate."

Axel frowned. "What's wrong?"

"She fainted. She was probably overwhelmed she had her first period. She's been worried because she hadn't had it yet and there's no one to talk to about it. She passed out from the sight of blood and cut her arm on a metal grate in the bathroom when she passed out."

"Oh, I see."

Betty nodded. "She said they taught it in school, but for a young girl without a mom, it can still be a shock. I know I had a similar uncomfortable conversation with my father when it happened to me."

Axel scrubbed a hand over his face. "I should've prepared her better, but…"

"I get it."

"Did she tell you what happened?" Axel asked cautiously. "About her father?"

Betty nodded. "She did."

Axel seemed uncertain.

"I asked her what happened to her parents. She told me."

"Of course, I'm sorry. It was hard for me and I've been trying to be there for her and apparently what I've been doing is not good enough."

"It's good enough."

He shot her a disbelieving stare. "Well, I'm glad she was able to confide in you."

"I told her that if she had any more questions she could ask me. I hope I didn't overstep my boundaries."

"No, but I don't want her burdening you either. You have a job to do," he said quickly.

"It's not a burden. I know the special circumstances of the situation she's going through."

Axel cocked an eyebrow. "How so?"

"My mother died shortly after I was born and it was just me and my father after my grandmother died when I was a bit older than Eira. It's hard and you shouldn't be so tough on yourself. You're doing a good job."

"You've only just met me. You have no concept about whether or not I'm doing a good job."

It was a snarky retort, but she couldn't blame him. They were still strangers and he'd been through a lot.

"I'm going to get her what she needs and suture her wound. You should take her home and watch for signs of infection."

Axel nodded, but he didn't look at her.

She turned to walk away and he reached out and touched her arm.

"I'm sorry for snapping. Thank you."

She smiled. "You're welcome, Dr. Sturlusson."

She turned and left him standing there. She had a newfound appreciation for him. He still might be closed off, but at least she understood that it was because he'd been through the wringer himself and for that she could cut him a little bit of slack.

But only a little.

CHAPTER FOUR

WHAT AM I DOING?

She stared up at the gray door of a modern-looking house in a posh area of Reykjavik.

Everything about it screamed clean and orderly. The house was definitely Axel's, as his SUV was in the driveway. Eira had left a notebook in the emergency room yesterday. It must've slipped from her backpack and Betty wanted to return it.

She closed her eyes, hesitating briefly and thinking about running in the opposite direction, but she mustered her courage and knocked.

She didn't like visiting people without an invitation, but she wanted to return Eira's homework and to check up on her.

She was worried about Eira because she knew how Eira felt. She'd been that frightened teenaged girl with no woman to talk to.

And she was worried that Eira might not tell her uncle if she was feeling crampy or even if she had a fever.

Betty had convinced herself it was best if she personally checked on Eira.

The door opened and a confused Axel answered. He was in denim, a flannel shirt and he had glasses on.

The sight of him made her heart skip a beat. Dammit, he was just as handsome in his casual attire as he was in scrubs.

"Dr. Jacinth?" he asked, taking the glasses off and tucking them in the front pocket of his shirt.

"You can call me Betty when we're not at the hospital."

He didn't acknowledge that. "What're you doing here?"

"I brought some food and some other things for Eira. I wanted to check on her."

Axel stepped to the side, silently inviting her in. She stepped into the foyer. It was minimalistic and gray. Cool shades rather than colors, but there was also a strange warmth to the place.

"How did you get here?"

"I took a cab."

He frowned. "If you'd called I could have come and gotten you."

Betty handed him the bag of food she'd brought and slipped off her boots.

"I'm used to taking cabs. I'm from New York City."

"So you keep reminding me."

"Besides, how could I call when I didn't know your phone number?"

"Ah, but you found out where I lived." There was a sly smile on his face.

Damn. He had a point.

"You might've not answered a strange number. I wouldn't have." She held out the notebook. "Eira left this in the emergency room."

"Well, it doesn't matter now because you're here." He set the bag on the floor and then took her coat. "Eira is on the sofa watching television, unless she drifted off to sleep again. I'll take this to the kitchen."

"All except this bag." Betty took back the bag of things she had bought specifically for Eira. Private things that her uncle didn't need to see. It was chocolates, feminine hygiene products and other things to make Eira smile. The other bag was food, everything to make a pizza, which had always been Betty's comfort food.

Axel nodded in understanding and then pointed. "The living room is just through that way."

"Thanks." Betty made her way to the sunken living room. On a large sectional couch Eira was propped up in the corner, with brightly covered quilts, a little tray with some food and her laptop. It was chaos and color in the midst of the cool gray and minimalistic decor of the room.

Eira brightened up. "Dr. Jacinth!"

"Betty."

"Betty," Eira said. "What're you doing here?"

"I wanted to check on you and bring you some more things that I think that you might need." She handed the bag to Eira and the girl peeked inside. "There's also some not so needed things in there. Some nice stuff to brighten your day."

"Thank you!" Eira said.

"You also forgot this." Betty handed her the notebook. "How is your pain?"

"Not bad, but I've been shivering. Can't get warm."

Betty frowned and picked up the thermometer that was on the table. She stuck it in Eira's ear and it beeped, showing a fever.

Axel came into the room and frowned. "She has a fever?"

"Yes." Betty set the thermometer down. "Can I check your wound?"

Eira nodded. Betty used some hand sanitizer from her bag and pulled back the gauze. It was still red and angry, but she could see signs of infection starting.

"I'll prescribe her some antibiotics."

"You won't have a prescription pad yet." Axel crossed the room and pulled a pad out of a desk, where a laptop sat. He wrote something out. "I'll call this in and have the pharmacy deliver it."

"I think you should probably go to bed," Betty said to Eira.

"Yeah. I'm tired and achy."

Betty helped Eira up and carried the blankets and other things to her room. She helped Eira get settled in bed and then headed back downstairs. Axel was cleaning up the tray.

"How is she?" he asked.

"Tired. Wake her up to get her started on the antibiotics. I gave her a tetanus shot at the hospital so you don't have to worry about that."

"I know. I read her chart before we left."

"You didn't trust me." And that irked her because it reminded her of Thomas and how he'd always been checking on her every move. Picking at everything. She'd thought it was because he cared for her. How wrong she'd been.

Axel set the tray back down. "I don't know you, Betty. And Eira is my responsibility."

"I know. And look, I'm sorry about…"

He held up a hand. "I'd rather not talk about it."

The tension in the room was thick and Betty felt bad for broaching the subject.

"Well, I better go."

"No, stay a while. I have to wait until the pharmacy delivers Eira's antibiotics and then I can drive you home. It'll be a couple of hours— the least I could do is make you dinner with the food you brought."

"You don't have to do that."

She wasn't here to make friends.

She wasn't here to get entangled with another man. All she wanted to do tonight was bring Eira some things she would need and then leave.

"Please," Axel said. "I would like you to stay."

The invitation caught him off guard. He couldn't believe he was doing it, but then again he couldn't believe she'd come to check on Eira. That had surprised him. Most women he met didn't want the burden of dating a sullen surgeon with a teenage niece who was his sole responsibility.

And anyone that couldn't accept Eira and his duty to her and Calder, Axel didn't want to be around. So it shocked him that Betty cared so much.

That Betty had even showed up.

He knew he should send her away because he didn't deserve her company or her compassion, but there was a part of him that was lonely and welcomed her company.

Especially tonight. After his father had found out what had happened to Eira, he had lit into Axel. Blaming Axel for not recognizing the signs.

"It was a good thing someone with sense was there and able to take care of Eira properly."

What he should've done was told his father off, pointed out the fact that he had been the one to step up and take care of Eira when his father couldn't. Axel had lost someone too but still he soldiered on.

You haven't really grieved.

Axel shook the unexpected thought away. There was no place for grief in his life. He didn't have time to grieve. He had to keep moving forward. For Eira.

"Please stay, Betty."

"Okay. I'd like that."

"Have a seat and I'll get you something to drink. Would you like wine or tea?"

"Wine would be great."

He nodded and headed into the kitchen. He pulled down a couple of wine glasses and pulled out the only bottle of white wine that he had in the fridge. Entertaining was very low on his priority list.

He uncorked it and poured two glasses. When he went into the other room Betty was standing in the dining area, staring out over the night sky. His house was perched on top of a hill with a great view over the city.

"Here you are," he said, handing her the glass.

"Thank you. You have a beautiful view. Can you see the water from here?"

"Yes," he replied tightly. "Although this isn't really my house. It was my brother's."

"Oh, I thought it was yours. It seemed to suit you."

"Well, Calder was a lot like me. He was my older brother and I looked up to him. I was just living in a small flat. I thought it would

be best for Eira to stay in her own house instead of trying to move her whole life into my
one-room flat."

"That makes sense." She took a sip of wine
and silence fell between them again. She
glanced over at the computer. "What're you
working on?"

"The surgical training program for next
year. I'm responsible for hiring the surgical
interns. I go through their CVs, basically. My
father wants me to be more involved in the
hospital."

"That sounds...fun? You don't sound too
enthused."

"I'm not," Axel sighed. "My father insists,
though."

"What do you want to do at the hospital?"

"Save lives. Before...before the accident I
had plans to sub-specialize in cardiothoracic
surgery, but I've had Eira and the ER taking
up all my time since my brother died."

Betty nodded. "Sub-specializing is smart. I
studied laparoscopic surgery in my fourth year
of residency. I'm quite a wizard when it comes
to laparoscopic procedures."

"Really?" he asked, intrigued.

She nodded. "It's what I'm teaching the first-
year residents."

"They're lucky to learn from you."

She blushed and smiled. "Thanks."

He liked when she smiled. "Why did you accept this job? I looked you up when my father announced you'd accepted the job—you had a very prominent position at that hospital."

A strange expression crossed her face.

"Yes, well… I was under-appreciated."

He knew how that felt. "So you felt coming to Reykjavik was a good move?"

"It might shake up the board having me gone. Perhaps they'll learn to appreciate me more." She turned and looked away. He could tell by the way her brow was furrowed and the way her body had tensed that there was more to it than that.

"Let's have something to eat. I didn't eat much today since I had to leave work early because of Eira."

"That sounds great."

They wandered into the kitchen and Betty helped him as he laid out bread and cheese.

"What did you bring? I put the stuff away, but the tomato sauce and flatbread was an odd choice," he said.

"I couldn't find the right crust."

He cocked an eyebrow. "Crust?"

"Yeah, for Eira," Betty said.

There was obviously some language barrier because he didn't understand what she was trying to explain to him.

"Eira's not a fan of flatbread and tomato sauce. I don't think she's had it before."

"I didn't know what she liked. If she was a fourteen-year-old in New York I might've brought her a slice."

"A slice of what?" Now he was really confused.

"Pizza," she said, smiling. "I didn't know which pizza place here was good, though."

Axel chuckled as he realized she'd brought the ingredients for pizza. "This is fine, but for future reference there is a little Italian place not far from where you live. Antonio's. It has the best Italian food and Eira is a big fan."

"That's good to know."

Axel cut her a piece of bread while she sliced the cheese. She made up a sandwich for him and then one for herself. They put them on plates and took them into the living room, sitting on the couch in front of the fire.

They said nothing as they enjoyed the fire and their food.

It was nice.

"How was the rest of the day?" he asked, breaking the silence that had fallen between them. "I was supposed to work and help you, but I had to stay with Eira today."

"Nothing that eventful happened. I didn't make it into the operating room today. It was pretty routine, but I also think that was by your father's design."

"What was?" asked Axel.

"I think he had me on a light duty today. Not that I blame him, my body is still getting used to the time zone change. I suspect that tomorrow will be different, but I need some time to get ready for my first lecture with your surgical residents at the end of the week. I'm a bit nervous about that."

"Why? You worked in a teaching hospital in New York, did you not?"

"I did, but I didn't really work with the interns or residents much. My department head did that mostly."

And there it was again, that bitterness when she mentioned her department head and the former hospital she worked at. What had that department head done to hurt Betty? Was he the reason she'd left New York?

It couldn't be that. She wasn't staying in Reykjavik permanently.

The doorbell rang.

"That must be the antibiotics. Excuse me."

Axel left and retrieved the medicine, paying the driver. He shut the door and saw Betty in the foyer.

"I should get back to my place. I'm exhausted and if I'm going to get used to this new time, I should go to sleep at a reasonable hour."

"Let me just give Eira a dose and I'll drive you."

"Don't worry, I called a cab and he's here."

Axel glanced out of the front window and saw the cab waiting on the street.

"Are you sure?"

"Positive." Betty pulled on her boots and then her coat. "I'll see you tomorrow at the hospital. I think I can make my own way over there."

Axel nodded. "Okay. See you tomorrow."

He opened the door and watched Betty get into the cab and then watched it drive her away.

It was nice spending the evening with her. It was unexpected, but, as nice as it was, it couldn't continue.

There was a time limit to her being here and this was where his life was.

He had to remember to keep his distance,

even if every fiber of his being wanted something completely different when it came to Dr. Betty Jacinth.

CHAPTER FIVE

Betty walked through the halls of the hospital on her way to the surgical floor to remove a gallbladder from a patient who had come in during the early hours of the morning, right before the shift change, complaining of pain.

Betty could see the patient was jaundiced and because the bilirubin in the patient's blood was high it was clear that the pancreas was taking over. If they didn't do a cholecystectomy soon then the patient would be prone to pancreatitis, which was way worse.

She hadn't done a surgery in a couple of weeks and she was looking forward to getting into the operating room and showing all these skeptical surgeons in Reykjavik that she had the skills. That they could trust her.

The quiet of the operating room, focusing on a procedure she'd done countless times before, would also help her get her mind off Axel.

She hadn't intended to stay, but she was lonely. She'd only been in Iceland for a week and she was having a hard time handling the solitude.

It's been more than a week. You've been lonely since your father died.

She shook that thought away as she stopped just outside the door to the surgical floor. Here she changed her lab coat for a surgical gown, placed booties over her shoes and tied back her hair, putting on her surgical scrub cap that she'd brought with her from New York.

It was pink and had hearts on it. It made her happy, but the moment she pulled it on all the other stoical surgeons that were in that room stared at her.

She realized that they all had the same scrub cap. That aqua blue that matched their scrubs.

Great.

She tried to ignore the pointed stares as she continued getting ready to perform her surgery.

"Well, if you wanted to disrupt the flow of the surgical floor I would say mission accomplished."

She turned around to see Axel leaning beside her, grinning. He was thoroughly amused and just that grin on his face made her heart skip a beat, her palms clammy. Suddenly she was nervous around him and she could recall her dreams from last night vividly, because they had been filled with Axel. She'd enjoyed her time with him over this last week. And she loved the way he was with his niece. That made her just swoon. It took a strong man to step up and take care of a teenager like that. Especially while simultaneously balancing a demanding career.

But she had to stop thinking about that.

That was why she was looking forward to the silence and focus of the operating room.

"You think it's funny?" she asked.

"I like seeing them shaken up a bit. And the scrub cap suits you."

"What?"

"It's whimsical. I don't know, it suits you. Makes you stand out."

"I didn't really expect to stand out today. I thought…"

"What did you think?" he asked.

"I thought it would be like the hospital in New York. We all have our little personal scrub caps."

"It's nice."

She narrowed her eyes. "You're being awfully nice to me today."

"There's a reason."

"Oh?" she asked, intrigued.

"I would like to get in on your surgery."

"It's just an emergency cholecystectomy. I'm sure you've done many before."

"I have, but I haven't done one with you. I am your mentor while you're here and I would like to assist. You say you're a wizard with the laparoscope."

Her stomach twisted and she couldn't help but think of Thomas.

It's not like that.

"I see. You're observing the new girl."

"Something like that."

Well, that explained his friendlier attitude. He was buttering her up and she seriously doubted he would listen if she said no anyway. He was going to assist whether she liked it or not.

"Do I have a choice?" she asked.

"Not really," he admitted.

"Then I would love to have you," she said, faking an enthusiasm she didn't feel. Honestly, she didn't want him anywhere near her surgery. What if he took over as Thomas had? Maybe he wouldn't, but she couldn't be sure of anything.

Axel smiled at her. "I'll see you in a few moments."

Betty nodded and stepped through the doors onto the sterile surgical floor. She found the scrub room that was attached to her operating room and began her scrubbing. As she glanced through the window into the operating room where the patient was being prepped she saw that there was a gallery and that that gallery was filled with surgeons. Including the senior Dr. Sturlusson.

Her heart began to pound. She was suddenly nervous.

You wanted to prove to them you're good. You want them to trust you. This is how.

She took a deep breath. It definitely was the way to do it, but there was a part of her that still felt like the second wheel behind Thomas, as she'd been in New York.

You've got this. You can do this.

"Let me lead this one, Betty," Thomas had said.

"It's my patient," she'd argued.

"Yes, but the board is here tonight to see me do a surgery after my stellar diagnosis of the director of the board's wife. I'm the one to watch for Head of General Surgery." He'd touched her cheek. "And of course you'll be at my side, assisting me. I couldn't do it without you."

Her heart had skipped a beat.

"Okay... And then maybe tonight we can get a drink and celebrate?"

"Sure..."

Of course there had been no celebration. He'd abandoned her for others and she'd felt the fool giving up her surgery for him because she'd thought it would make Thomas care about her more. That if she'd said no to him he'd reject her and yet he'd rejected her anyways.

Her stomach twisted.

This was different. Axel might be assisting with her surgery but he wasn't taking it over. So why did she still feel as if she was being pushed aside? Insignificant again.

Axel entered the scrub room and stood beside her at the sink, scrubbing in. She glanced up at him and instantly all the thoughts about Thomas, the self-doubt that he made her feel, melted away.

This was different.

"I apparently have quite the audience in the gallery."

"Everyone is eager to see how you perform,

Dr. Jacinth. That's all. Your reputation precedes you."

"What reputation?" she asked.

"You are well respected in New York. My father is a smart man—he wouldn't have had just anyone come to teach his surgical residents for several months."

"You flatter me." She shot him a smile.

"Well, we'll see how you do out there." Axel winked and dried his hands, heading out into the operating room.

Betty took another deep breath.

This was just like every other cholecystectomy. She could do this. She dried her hands and headed out into the operating room. A scrub nurse helped her on with her gown and she glanced up briefly at the crowd in the gallery.

You've got this.

She nodded to Axel's father and then tried to forget that he was there. That she was under a microscope here in the operating room.

She took her spot at the operating table and Axel stood on the other side of her. He nodded and she could tell from the crinkle in the corner of his eye that he was smiling at her from behind his surgical mask.

Yeah, she had this.

* * *

Betty was still dictating her surgical report in the operating room. Axel had just finished scrubbing out, eager to get home and check on Eira. He'd had their neighbor, Mrs. Ingborne, sitting with her this morning while he was at the hospital. Mrs. Ingborne had raised ten healthy children and, as she often watched Eira when Calder had to work, he knew his niece was in good hands.

Still, Axel needed to get home to check on her for himself. When he'd entered that operating room he had caught his father's eye and seen the look of displeasure. He'd known exactly what his father was thinking. That he didn't want Axel in the operating room.

"I'm surprised to see you here, Axel," his father said stiffly.

"I was surprised to see you and so many others in the gallery. Why such a packed gallery for a simple cholecystectomy procedure?"

"The board was curious about how well Dr. Jacinth would perform and whether or not she was just as capable as her father. He was a brilliant surgeon. He worked here in this hospital for some time."

Axel raised his eyebrows. "So I've heard."

"Well, that's why I wanted Clifford Jacinth's

daughter to lead our interns in their last few months with us. I'm hoping that she will pick out the best and the brightest. Her father had quite the knack for it."

Betty hadn't gone into much detail about her father or his reputation for being such a brilliant surgeon, but then again Axel hadn't really asked her for details.

And the reason he hadn't was because he'd wanted to keep her at arm's length. The problem was, he kept getting sucked back in. Why couldn't he just leave Betty alone?

Why did he have to be the surgeon to show her the ropes here?

Because you're the lowest on the totem pole here. Even Betty outranks you.

He knew his place in the hierarchy was because of his father and not because of his skills as a surgeon. Axel also had the feeling, by the way the other surgeons were looking at Betty—as if she was an interloper who didn't belong—that no one else had wanted the job of helping her settle in.

They were missing out. She was a talented surgeon. Two minutes into the surgery and he'd known that. Watching her operate had been awe-inspiring.

She had a level of skill he hadn't seen since Calder.

"She did very well on the surgery. Perhaps you'll start giving her more time in the operating room now?" It was a dig at his father for not allowing Betty to have operating-room privileges from day one and the expression on the older man's face made it clear his father knew it.

"Of course. How is Eira today?"

"She has a mild infection. She's on a course of antibiotics for another couple of days."

"She has an infection and you left her at home, alone?" his father asked. "You should be with her."

"I am a surgeon, Father. I do have to work. Besides, she's been on antibiotics for a week and I've already taken time off to care for her, or have you forgotten?"

"Eira should be your priority."

"She is." Axel clenched his fists at his sides and tried to count back from ten; the anger he had to keep in check around his father was exhausting. "You want me here doing more and striving for more, yet you want me at home with all my attention focused on Eira. I can't do both."

His father ignored him. "I don't see how Eira

can be a priority when you're here and she's by herself at home."

"She's not by herself. Mrs. Ingborne is watching her until I can finish my work and get home. Perhaps you could stop by and visit your granddaughter? See for yourself how she's doing?"

His father's eyes narrowed. Axel had hit another sore spot.

Axel knew it was hard for his father to be around Eira—he reminded his father of Calder and Axel's late mother—but that was no excuse for never seeing her. Axel wanted to believe that deep down his father really loved Eira, but he knew it was a lie he'd been telling himself over and over again for years.

"If time allows me, I will," his father said. "I'd better check on the board of directors. Please pass on my congratulations to Dr. Jacinth."

Axel watched his father storm down the hallway. Taking a deep breath, he left the operating-room floor and headed back to the charge room, pulling off his scrub cap and tossing it into a laundry bin.

Betty followed him through the door, pulling off her scrub cap and sticking it in her bag in her locker.

Axel cocked an eyebrow.

"I have a feeling it won't come back if I send it to the laundry here. I'll just take it home and wash it myself and then stick to the regulation ones for the next couple of months."

"Don't give up so easily. I like your scrub cap."

She smiled and shook her head. "It's better to blend in sometimes."

"Yeah, but it's also good to stand out."

"This is strange talk coming from you."

"What do you mean?"

"The first time I met you, you nagged me about the inappropriate footwear I was wearing and how it didn't conform to what you felt was appropriate footwear."

"Well, you did slip," he reminded her.

She crossed her arms. "It was icy."

"And that was my point all along." He was teasing her and he enjoyed it.

"Ha. Ha." She pulled on her lab coat. "Back down to the pit."

"The pit?"

"It's what we call the emergency room back in New York."

"I'll walk down with you, if you don't mind."

"Sure."

They were silent as they fell into step, side

by side as they walked from the operating floor to the emergency room.

"Would you like to come over to dinner tonight?" The question caught him off guard because it had been a long time since he'd asked a woman out to dinner.

"Sure." Betty sounded stunned.

"I'll cook. I do cook, though it didn't appear like I did when I made you sandwiches instead of pizza, which Eira loved, by the way."

"Good to know and I would like that."

"I'll drive you home and then we can go back to my place."

"I have *got* to get a car," she teased. "I can't rely on you to drive me everywhere."

"I don't mind. My father said you were my responsibility. I want to make sure that you're safe."

"And is that why you're inviting me to dinner?" she asked. "Because I'm just a responsibility?"

"Partly." He was honest about it. "But also Eira does like you. I'm glad that you were there to talk to her about everything. And even though she's suffering through that and an infection, she's been quite pleasant the last couple of days."

Betty grinned. "I would like to see Eira again.

She's a sweetheart and I guess I feel a connection to her because I know what she's feeling."

He nodded. "By the way, my father wanted me to pass on his congratulations."

She raised her eyebrows. "Seems strange for a routine surgery."

"Yes, it does."

Only he understood. It might have been a routine surgery, but apparently Betty wasn't a routine surgeon. She was the daughter of someone his father admired and that meant something. His father was not someone who gave his admiration away freely.

"I'll meet you at the front doors of the hospital at six."

He turned and walked away, heading to his assigned pod.

He didn't know what he was doing inviting her to dinner.

It's for Eira.

And that was what he had to keep telling himself, but he knew that wasn't completely true.

He didn't want to face the real truth. The truth that she fascinated him, she was attractive, funny, smart and feisty.

He wanted to get to know her better. Even though he knew there was a time limit on anything they might share, even though he knew he didn't deserve happiness. He came with too much baggage. No one deserved to bear that burden but him. Happiness wasn't for him.

He didn't deserve it at all.

CHAPTER SIX

AFTER HER SHIFT FINISHED, Betty quickly changed out of her scrubs. In New York, the doctors' locker room had always been filled with lively banter. But here, Betty got changed in silence. She wasn't making many friends here in Reykjavik. It was as if the other surgeons saw her as an interloper and she'd only been here for a week.

This was not boding well for the next eighty-seven days. That was why she was clinging to the only branch of friendship she was being offered. She was just surprised it was coming from Axel. When she'd first met him, he'd been so closed off, so grumpy, but there was more to him than that first meeting, as she was discovering.

Usually when she had to work with a new surgeon during a surgery there was a learning curve. Even with experienced surgeons. If two surgeons hadn't worked together before, they were unfamiliar with each other's techniques.

And accomplished surgeons were usually stuck in their way. Unyielding and unbending.

Yet, Axel hadn't given her a hard time. He'd worked with her so well. It was as if they had been working together for a long time.

The last time she'd had that kind of rapport with another surgeon…well, she didn't want to think about *him*. He was the reason she was here in Iceland.

She was falling into the old trap. Her relationship with Thomas had started similarly, except he hadn't had a niece and he hadn't survived a traumatic accident that claimed the life of his beloved brother. It had just started with them working together on a surgery, followed by an invitation to dinner to celebrate.

"You ready?"

Betty turned around and her heart skipped a beat. Axel was standing behind her and he was in his street clothes. Even in tailored pants and a sweater he looked as if he'd stepped out of a magazine.

And suddenly she felt a bit dowdy in her jeans, cotton tee shirt and big clunky boots.

"You look nice," she said.

"So do you."

"Liar."

He grinned, his blue eyes twinkling. "No, I mean it. I really like the boots. They're practical."

She rolled her eyes. "Let's go."

They walked out to his SUV. Snow was falling thickly and she shivered as she zipped up her parka.

"The streets might be a bit dicey tonight," Axel said.

"We can always cancel. I can catch a cab and you can get home to Eira."

"No, it'll be fine," he said tightly. Somehow she got the feeling that it wasn't fine, that he was worried about something.

She hoped he wasn't regretting his invitation for her to join him for dinner. Of course, if that was the case he would've just taken her home, wouldn't he?

As they pulled out onto the Hverfisgata, the SUV wheels spun slightly in the snow. It was slippery out tonight. Black ice under a sheet of fresh snow probably meant there was disaster lurking.

Don't think about that.

It was bad luck to think about impending doom, especially when you worked in emergency medicine.

"I'm going to save you tonight."

"What?" Betty asked, confused.

"I ordered some take-out from Antonio's. We'll pick up the order and then head back to my place. I hope you don't mind."

"Not at all. I guess I'll get a taste of Reykjavik's version of the best pizza."

"It's not flatbread," Axel teased and she couldn't help but laugh.

"Oh, good, because I'm particular about my pizza."

"Really?" he asked.

"I live in New York. Nothing beats a New York City slice."

Axel smiled at her. "I think you'll like Antonio's pizza."

"You're putting a lot of pressure on Antonio," Betty teased. "It's a lot to live up to."

"I think you'll like it."

Axel parked in front of Antonio's and he ran inside while Betty waited in his SUV. She watched the snow falling steadily; it was almost hypnotic.

He came out a few moments later and placed the food in the back seat. The moment she caught the scent of it her stomach let out a growl of hunger.

"Sorry about that," she said, embarrassed. "It's been a while since I last ate."

"We'll take care of it soon."

Axel's house wasn't far from Antonio's. Once they'd parked, Betty climbed out of the car and followed Axel into the house. Eira was up and sitting on the couch. She completely perked up when she saw that he was carrying take-out bags.

"You got Antonio's?" Eira asked eagerly. Then Eira saw Betty. "Betty! I'm so glad to see you."

"I'm glad to see you too. You look better."

"I'm feeling better."

"Are you hungry?" Axel asked.

"Starving." Eira took the bags from her uncle and carried them into the kitchen. Betty took off her boots and hung up her coat.

"I'll help Eira," Betty offered.

"No, you're our guest. Have a seat in the dining room and I'll make you up a plate." Axel disappeared into the kitchen and Betty made her way into the dining room. She took a seat and Eira quickly set the table and then Axel brought out the food.

It was pizza and it looked like what she was used to. It was pretty informal as they passed around the food and began to eat.

It was nice. It was homey and for the first time in a long time she felt as if she belonged. It also made her feel lonely, because this could never be a permanent thing. She was here to work, to prove herself and then she would be leaving.

There was nothing permanent about her stay in Iceland.

Once dinner was finished, Betty helped Axel clean up and Eira went to bed. It was quiet in the house and it was different without Eira there to break the tension between them.

"Thank you for dinner tonight," Betty said as she dried a dish. "I appreciated it."

"You're welcome and thank you again for your help with Eira."

"My pleasure." She looked up at him, his blue eyes locked on her and her pulse kicked up a notch. She was so close to him and he was making her weak in the knees. She had to get out of here. She looked away and cleared her throat. "I should probably get home. Would you like me to call a cab?"

"Right." Axel nodded. "I can take you. The roads are treacherous. I'll just leave a note letting Eira know I'm taking you home in case she wakes up."

"Okay."

* * *

The car ride back to her place was quiet and awkward. Or maybe it was just her feeling that way. She had rushed him to get out of the door, because she wanted to put space between them, because she didn't like the direction they were heading. It wasn't that it was unwelcome; it was just that she couldn't date a colleague. She refused to ever do that again.

They stopped at a light and just before she was about to ask Axel why he'd asked her over for dinner tonight, because it was clear something had changed between them, a car came careening across the intersection, T-boning a truck, which sent the truck spiraling toward them.

It happened so fast, but everything seemed to go in slow motion as Betty closed her eyes as the SUV spun around and ended up facing the opposite direction they had been heading in.

Once the SUV stopped, she opened her eyes and through the thick falling snow she could see fire and destruction.

"Axel?" she cried out, turning to look at him.

He was staring out of his window, his hands gripping the wheel.

"Are you okay?" Betty asked.

"Yeah, are you?"

"I'm fine, just shaken up."

Axel nodded. "Call emergency services. I'm going to go out and help."

Betty nodded and pulled out her cell phone. "Wait, I don't know where we are!"

And even if she knew where she was she wasn't completely sure that she'd be able to say the name of the intersection correctly.

Axel rolled his eyes and called the emergency number, giving their location and details of the crash. When he was done he handed her phone back and went to the trunk of his SUV, pulling out a bag.

Betty climbed out of the SUV and saw the front end was crushed from where they had been hit.

They were lucky that nothing all that bad had happened to them.

"Betty, you're bleeding!" Axel tilted her chin and she touched her head, seeing blood on her fingers. There was concern in his eyes and his hand was gentle on her face.

"It's just a scratch."

"It could be more. Why don't you sit in the SUV and wait?"

"Or it's just a scratch. I want to help and you need help," she said. "I'm fine."

Axel nodded. "Let's go."

Betty had done training for emergency situations like this, but she had never experienced actually being at the scene. Usually she was in the emergency room waiting for the ambulance to come in.

Axel approached the burning truck and the lone occupant who had been ejected through the front window.

It didn't look good as Axel knelt down and did a quick assessment. He pulled out an emergency blanket to cover the victim. Betty moved toward the car that had T-boned the truck.

There were other people milling about and helping a hysterical woman, who had a large head wound and was cradling a crying child.

"Ma'am, I'm a doctor. Can I help?" The woman shook her head, not understanding Betty's English. So Betty repeated it in Icelandic.

"I don't know what happened," the hysterical woman cried out. "I just lost control coming down the hill."

"It's okay, ma'am. Can I check your head wound?"

The woman nodded and sat down in the car via the open door of her vehicle.

Betty pulled out a small flashlight she had in her bag to examine the wound. It was deep and it would need stitches; the woman's nose also appeared to be broken.

"Can I see your baby?" Betty asked.

The woman nodded and handed her baby over to Betty. Thankfully there was nothing wrong with the baby, it was just scared and crying. Betty could see the infant carrier in the back seat. It had done its job.

The sound of sirens cut through the cold night air, followed by the blare of a firetruck.

The first ambulance parked near Axel and his patient on the ground. The second ambulance parked near her. A paramedic came toward her.

"Do you speak English?" Betty asked him. He nodded.

"Patient has a deep laceration to the forehead and a possible fracture of the septum."

"Are you a doctor?" the paramedic asked.

"I am. I've been here a week."

"You're American?"

"Yes."

The paramedic smiled brightly. He was handsome with blond hair and blue eyes.

"It's a pleasure to meet you. We've got the patient from here."

Betty nodded and stepped back to let the paramedics do their work.

She looked over her shoulder and could see Axel helping the paramedics load his patient into the ambulance.

The fire was being put out by the firemen and a police officer was waiting to talk to Axel.

She walked over to them, but the closer she got, the more the scent of acrid smoke from the burning car made her stomach dizzy. In fact, the whole world was spinning a little out of control.

"Betty?" Axel asked, alarmed.

"I'm…" Only she couldn't finish that sentence as the world began spinning faster and she felt her knees give out from underneath her.

He was carrying her again. Only this time she wasn't protesting and he kind of missed that.

Axel wished she were fighting him now, instead of lying unconscious in his arms. Blood on her pale face.

He should've made her stay in the SUV. He shouldn't have let her work with him. She'd been bleeding and he should've known better. Should have known it was just adrenaline when she stated that she was fine.

And when the adrenaline had worn out, she'd collapsed.

Axel carried her through the doors of the emergency room and the doctors on duty looked at him in shock as he carried her through the triage area, straight to a private exam room.

His father came into the exam room, shutting the door behind him.

"What happened?"

"A car T-boned another truck, which sent that vehicle into mine. Betty sustained a small laceration to the head, but I think she may have a concussion. She passed out shortly after she triaged some of the injured on-scene."

His father sighed. "I'll take care of her. One of your patients is in the next exam room."

Axel nodded. He didn't want to leave Betty, but he wanted to check on the young man who he had triaged in the field. The one that had been thrown from his truck.

As he moved toward the other exam room Axel pulled off his coat and slipped into a surgical gown. One of the head residents was working on his patient.

"I'll take over."

The resident nodded. Axel could tell from the grim expression on the resident's face that it was not good, but Axel wasn't going to give up yet.

He wasn't going to lose this young man.

Not the way he'd lost Calder.

Hang on. Just hang on.

As he worked over the young man, he couldn't help but think about Betty too. How she'd been injured and how it had scared him to see her crumple like that. It was all he could do to reach forward and catch her before her head had hit the cold, icy road.

He shouldn't have let her work. She had been bleeding. He should've known better.

Don't think about it.

Instead he focused on his patient. A young man who hadn't been wearing a seat belt in bad weather. He quickly intubated the man and continued focusing on keeping his heart pumping.

"Hold on, Calder."

His brother moaned, his eyes closed, his lips blue. "Can't."

"Hold on!"

The monitor flatlined after several attempts of reviving his patient and trying to stabilize him. Axel leaned over and checked his pupils.

Dammit.

"Pupils fixated and dilated." Axel cursed

under his breath. "Time of death, twenty-two hundred hours."

Axel pulled off his surgical gown and stuffed it in the waste receptacle. He had to get out of here. It was just too much. He was a surgeon. He was supposed to save lives.

Dammit.

So young. A patient that was so young like that shouldn't have died. It was a waste. A waste of life.

His father opened the door and slipped out of Betty's exam room.

"How is she?" Axel asked.

"It appears she has a mild concussion, but you know how hard concussions are to diagnose. She'll need to rest for a few days and she can't be alone."

"Are you thinking of admitting her?"

"What choice do I have?" His father ran a hand over his head. "It's a shame that she won't be able to deliver her first lecture, but her health is more important."

"It is." Even though he knew he shouldn't, that he should stop the next words coming out of his mouth, he couldn't help himself. "I'll watch her. I have the next couple of days off, so I will stay with her. Or rather, she can stay with me."

His father was shocked. "Really?"

"Yes. She is my responsibility and she shouldn't be alone. There is a guest room and she can stay there. Besides, Eira likes her."

What are you doing?

A strange expression crossed his father's face. It hardened. "This shouldn't have happened in the first place."

"I was giving her a ride home." He didn't bother telling his father about the fact he was taking Betty home after having had dinner with her.

"We were hit because of bad weather. Walking in a snow squall when she doesn't know the city isn't responsible so giving her a ride was the right thing to do."

His father grumbled under his breath. " Well, it is good of you to step up and take care of her."

"I don't mind."

His father nodded. "Just watch for signs of concussion."

"I will." Axel half expected his father to explain the signs of a concussion to him, but he didn't.

"What happened with your patient?" his father asked.

"We lost him," Axel responded grimly.

"That's too bad." His father turned and walked away. He didn't offer any kind of condolence. He didn't ask about how the patient had died. Instead he'd said, "That's too bad" in a cold, disinterested way that ticked Axel off no end.

Axel closed his eyes. Angry that his father was so cold to him.

He couldn't think about that now. He had to get Betty home and he would have to take a cab as his SUV was probably right now being towed to the repair shop, but at least he would be with her.

He knocked on her exam-room door.

"Come in," she said.

He opened the door and saw her reclined on the exam table, a bandage on her forehead from the laceration. "How is your head? Did you need stitches?"

"Sore and no. It was a minor laceration."

"And you might have a concussion."

"I might. I do have nausea. Is your father admitting me?"

"No."

"No? But I have to be monitored for the next forty-eight hours."

"I know. That's why you're coming home with me."

She wasn't sure that she'd heard him correctly.

It could be the concussion.

It had to be the concussion.

"What did you say?" she asked.

"You're going to come home with me," he said matter-of-factly and he crossed his arms in the way she was coming to learn meant he wasn't going to discuss the matter further.

And she didn't have it in her to argue with him.

"I need some things from my place though."

"I'll accompany you. I'll help you pack up what you need and then you can stay in the guest bedroom at my place until we're sure that you don't have a concussion."

"Okay." She touched her bandaged head; it throbbed. She closed her eyes and leaned her head back against the exam-room table.

"Are you okay, Betty?"

"Dizzy."

"I'll get you a wheelchair and we'll get you back to my place."

"That sounds good."

That sounds good?

"I'll be right back." Axel left the room and Betty let out the breath she'd been holding. She couldn't go and live with him for a couple of days. That was absolute madness. How hard had she hit her head?

And when she thought back on it, she remembered being cradled in his strong arms. The warmth of his body making her feel safe. Axel had carried her into the emergency room. He might drive her nuts, he might keep throwing walls up, but there was a tender side to him.

It was a nice offer for him to take her in.

It would be better staying at a house than a noisy hospital and eating hospital food. This didn't have to mean anything. They were friends. Besides, Eira would be there.

Nothing would happen.

And Betty would make damn sure of that.

CHAPTER SEVEN

"YOU REALLY NEED to stop carrying me around," Betty protested as Axel lifted her from the car, but without much conviction. She had been dizzy on the drive over from the hospital to her house. She wasn't sure that she would be able to walk up the steps of her place and then manage to rummage through her things to find what she needed to take over to Axel's house.

"I'm getting used to carrying you around. I don't mind it." And there was a funny look on his face, which made her blood heat and told her, yeah, he probably really didn't mind it at all. She really didn't mind it either, but she should.

This was not keeping her distance or keeping things at a professional level.

She cleared her throat as they passed through her front door. "You can put me down now."

"Right." He set her down and looked around the cottage. It was small, but it was homey. So different from the minimalistic, cool, modern house he lived in.

"This is nice," he said.

"It is. It's cozy and I like hearing the water at night too."

His spine straightened. "I forgot how close you are to the water."

"I'm sorry." She remembered how weird he'd got when she'd suggested going to the coffee hut on the pier and then the walk on the beach.

"For what?" he asked offhandedly, not looking at her. He was trying to brush it off, as if it didn't bother him. She knew that stance all too well. How many times had she given the brush-off when it came to people questioning her about Thomas?

She knew not to push the subject with him.

"Nothing," she said. She shuffled to the bedroom and could hear Axel trailing after her.

"Whoa," he said.

"What?" she asked, although she knew what he was referring to. She was a bit of a slob and the small bedroom looked as if it had succumbed to a clothing bomb when she'd opened her suitcase.

"I know. I know."

"Were you robbed?" he asked, humor in his voice as he looked around.

"Ha-ha."

"No, seriously?"

"No. I wasn't robbed. I just… I have a system. Disorganized chaos."

"Well, I'm glad you have a system."

"I promise I won't employ my system at your place."

He arched an eyebrow. "As long as you contain it to the guest bedroom, you can do what you like."

"Thank you."

"What do you want to pack?"

"I can pack."

"You just had a head injury. I can pack. I was in the navy. I'm efficient."

"Fine. I'll toss you things and you pack." She flung a shirt over her shoulder at him and he reached out and caught it in mid-air.

"Impressive." She handed him her computer tablet.

It lit up in his hand. "Dr. Thomas Welling?"

Now it was her turn to freak out slightly. "What?"

"There's a bunch of missed chats with this

Dr. Welling. Is he someone from your hospital?"

"Yes." She took the tablet back and powered it down. "It's probably nothing."

She didn't want to talk about Thomas. She was here to forget Thomas.

"He's just a surgeon in New York at the hospital I work at."

"Oh, I see. Perhaps it's important."

"Doubtful. I'll answer him later." She shoved her tablet into her purse.

"Okay," he said, giving her the same consideration that she had given him when he'd gotten testy about the water.

She appreciated it.

He continued to help her pack up in silence.

She was unnerved that Thomas had been constantly messaging her. She'd come to Iceland to put him behind her, but how could she do that when he was still contacting her?

"You ready?" Axel asked as he zipped up her luggage.

"I am."

He nodded. "I'll call another cab. You rest here. I'll come back when we're ready to go."

"Okay."

Axel left the room with the suitcase. Betty pulled out her tablet and powered it on.

The last message from Thomas popped up.

How can I reach you? I need you.

It made her stomach knot and she was angry at herself, but she couldn't respond.

She didn't want to respond.

So she powered off her tablet and slipped it back into her purse, hating herself for not being rid of him yet.

Betty got settled in at Axel's home. Eira was thrilled that they had a house guest and was in high spirits, her infection starting to clear up. She'd gotten up and saw the note and was worried that Axel had been late getting home.

Even though Betty felt a bit sick to her stomach still, it was nice to sit and watch some television with two other people. She was lonelier than she'd originally thought.

"It's getting late. How are you feeling?" Axel whispered and Betty looked over to see Eira had fallen asleep in the corner of the sectional couch.

"I'm a little dizzy, but, with that coffee you made me, I think I'll be up for a while. If you want to go to bed though, don't worry about me. I can get up the stairs fine."

"You're dizzy and you're my responsibility. And I'm not tired, but I'll take Eira off to bed and make us some tea."

She watched as Axel gingerly picked up Eira and carried her off to bed.

He wasn't gone long. "Would you like some tea?" he asked when he returned.

"Sure." She stood and followed him into the kitchen.

"Something is bothering you," she said. "Do you want to talk about it?"

Axel sighed as he switched on the kettle. "The patient in the accident, the one I attended to, didn't make it."

Her heart sank. "I'm sorry."

She knew the feeling of fighting so hard for a patient, and eventually losing that fight was hard. And she knew Axel had done everything he could to save that young man's life.

"If he had been wearing a seat belt, he would've had a better shot."

"The woman who hit him will be devastated. Her car went out of control on black ice. She had some lacerations, but she was fine and her baby was fine too."

"That's good. It's not the weather that kills people, but the way the driver can't adjust to the weather. Weather is finicky. One minute you're in calm waters and the next…" He trailed off and then cleared his throat. "What a night."

"I agree." She thought about that opened message from Thomas and it ate away at her. "Dr. Welling is my former boyfriend."

Axel cocked an eyebrow. "Oh?"

"We still work together," she said with a sigh of resignation as he handed her a cup of freshly brewed tea. "We're on the same surgical team. Both general surgeons. He's the head of our team."

"And he didn't want you coming to Iceland," Axel said, as if reading her mind.

"You got it." She set her tea down and leaned on the counter across from him. "He 'needs' me."

"Maybe he's still in love with you." Axel's gaze locked with hers, those brilliant blue eyes that took her breath away.

"No. He's not."

"How do you know?"

"Because he just got married to someone else."

"And he still needs you? He tells you this?"

Betty nodded. "So I'm ignoring him."

"Good for you. That at least explains why you came to work under my father's iron fist."

Betty laughed. "Oh, come on, your father isn't that bad. He's quite nice and harmless."

Axel snorted derisively and shot her a look of disbelief as he stood back up and dumped the rest of his tea into the sink.

"To outsiders, he's a positive kitten." He pulled down a glass.

"Need something stronger?" she asked.

He nodded. "Yes. I would offer you some, but you're recovering from a head injury and the alcohol will mess with your medication."

"Yes, Doctor." Betty sipped her tea as he poured himself a small tumbler of clear liquid. "What's that?"

"Reyka. It's vodka." He drank it straight.

"I'm impressed."

"By what?" he asked.

"I've never seen anyone shoot straight vodka back like that. Like it was smooth. Vodka is strong."

He grinned lazily at her. "When you're feeling better I'll take you out to a bar and you can have a bottle of Viking Gold or another beer we're famous for."

"And I'm sure it'll put me right under the table. I can't hold my liquor."

Axel chuckled. "Well, as soon as I know you're not concussed and you're not relying on painkillers for your laceration we're going to go have a beer. You and I."

The thought of going out with him thrilled her, but also scared her.

"You're such a fun girl, Betty," Thomas had said as they'd stood beside each other at the scrub sink.

"Thanks. I think you're pretty cool too." She hadn't been sure what he was after.

"Want to get a drink after work tonight?"

"I'm not much of a drinker," she'd said.

"Just a glass of wine. I know this great wine bar."

"Okay. Sure."

Thomas's eyes had twinkled at her in that dreamy way that had caused so many women in the hospital to swoon.

"In case you're not aware, I'm asking you out."

"What?"

"I'm asking you out on a date." He'd smiled at her, a dimple in his cheek.

"Oh!" A blush had tinged her cheeks...

And that had turned out well. She'd fallen into bed with Thomas that night and fallen deeply in love with a man who was two-timing her right from the very start. A man who held her back, but used her to move his own career forwards.

Betty cleared her throat. "Well, I'd better go to bed. Thanks for the tea."

"Do you want me to carry you?" Axel asked.

"No!" Betty almost shouted, then she winced. She couldn't look him in the eye. "I'm fine. Goodnight, Axel."

She ran from the kitchen, as fast as she dared.

She couldn't put herself in that kind of situation again. She wasn't going to date another colleague. Ever.

She just couldn't.

Axel had been the one who was tired, but here he was, standing in the dark staring out over Reykjavik. Or what he could see of Reykjavik thanks to the blowing snow. He took another sip of his vodka.

His mind was on that young man who had lost his life. And it was also on Calder. It had been a snowstorm like this that had crept up when they had been in the helicopter. It sent a chill down his spine as the wind shook the sides of the house. It was howling. It was un-forgiving.

And if he wasn't afraid of flying or the water he would seriously think about relocating to a warmer climate, inland and away from the sea. But he had Eira.

Eira had friends in Iceland and he couldn't take Eira away from his father. He was the only family they both had left. Eira's late mother had had no family.

Not that his father bothered much with Eira since Calder died.

Still, he couldn't take her away from the only country she knew, and there was something else. There was this irrational fear that left him anchored in this life. He just couldn't go forward. It was as if he were still drowning.

Axel cursed under his breath and set the empty glass down on a side table and wandered away from the snow storm. He glanced at the clock on the wall and saw that it was two in the morning. Not unusual for him.

He had a hard time sleeping most nights.

Nightmares haunted him.

Calder, unconscious in the water. Frozen and slipping from his grasp. He should've been the one who died. Not Calder.

He was single. He had no children.

It should've been him.

He crept up the stairs slowly and saw that Betty's door was open a crack. A street lamp was reflecting light through the venetian blinds. His blood heated as he looked at her, sleeping on her back. One leg under the thick down duvet and one leg out, a sock slipping from her foot.

He smiled.

She made his heart skip a beat. She made him forget that he was drowning on dry land. And Eira perked up around Betty. It was the first time in a long time that he had been able to truly relax and enjoy just spending a night at home, watching a movie.

Not that he could particularly recall the movie they had been watching—it had been something that Eira had been bugging him to see—but it was nice just to sit there and feel completely at peace. And to have Eira smile again. It had been so long since she'd properly smiled.

And that was because of Betty.

Since she'd arrived he hadn't thought so much about Calder. About the nightmare of losing him. The sound of an angry sea that was threatening to swallow them whole was just a dim memory. Betty was like this bright, albeit sometimes annoying, beam of light in his life.

Yeah, but she's leaving in three months. She's not here to stay.

And that realization sobered him up. He backed away from the door, shutting it quietly, and headed to his room at the far end of the hall.

He knew that he wouldn't be getting much sleep tonight. So instead he fired up his laptop and began to work on all the admin strative tasks that fell to a doctor. And maybe, just maybe he would eventually tire himself out enough to fall into a dreamless sleep.

Otherwise he knew he would dream about Betty, a woman he didn't deserve.

A woman he could never have.

CHAPTER EIGHT

"You sure you feel well enough to go to school?" Axel asked as Eira sat at the island counter eating a bowl of porridge. "Do you have everything you need?"

"I'm fine, Uncle Axel. I need to get back to school. I don't want to fall too behind."

A small smile quirked on his lips. "Well, I can drive you."

"I can take the bus." Eira finished her breakfast. "How is Betty?"

"Sleeping still. I'll check on her in a bit," he said tightly, because he didn't want to think about Betty at the moment. When he had finally fallen asleep he'd dreamed about her. He'd dreamed about her in his arms.

It was unnerving.

He took Eira's bowl and washed it.

"If she's up for it you should take her around Reykjavik and see the sights."

"She's supposed to be resting. That's why we're both off work."

"She's injured but you're off work?"

"She has to be watched for concussion and your grandfather gave me to time off to watch you."

"She watched television last night though," Eira stated.

Axel cocked an eyebrow. "And?"

"Those with concussions shouldn't watch television. They get headaches."

Axel chuckled. "And how do you know?"

"I've spent my whole life around doctors. You pick stuff up. Besides, we covered it in health class recently," Eira replied tartly.

"Still, if she doesn't have a concussion we should get back to work."

"No, Uncle. You should take her out and show her a good time." There was a smug smile on her sweet little face. A mischievous playful smile that reminded Axel of Calder.

"What're you implying?"

"Nothing. She's American and she's here only for a short time. I'm sure if Grandfather has his way, her time will be spent in the hospital and she won't get to see any of Iceland. Now's your chance. Go let loose. You're wound way too tight."

"What?" Axel asked, shocked.

"Wound too tight." Eira grinned and then gave him a kiss on the cheek. "I have my keys. I'll see you later."

Axel shook his head as the door shut in the distance. Since when had Eira become so self-assured? He couldn't remember the last time she'd been so bubbly and affectionate. *This* was the Eira he remembered.

The vivacious little girl with the red curls and her father's devil-may-care attitude. His brother had always been full of life. Wanting to live it to the fullest. It was what Axel had always striven for, emulating his older brother, but he'd never been able to live as footloose and fancy-free as his brother had.

His brother, and even his father, had very tall shadows and Axel could never quite step out of the darkness and into the light.

Maybe that's why you're so drawn to Betty? She's light.

"Good morning."

He turned around, surprised to see her. Her hair was done and she was dressed for the day. Except for the paper sutures holding her gash together and some bruising, she looked well.

She looked really well.

And then an image from his dream came

rushing to the forefront of his mind. Of her in his arms, her luscious red lips against his and his hands in her silken blonde hair.

"How are you feeling?" he asked, trying to dispel the erotic dream from his mind.

"Okay. Slight headache, but I'm not dizzy. I'm wondering if I should go back to work today."

"Don't push it. My father said you were to take two days off."

She crossed her arms. "I have a lot of work to do. I'm behind on preparing my lectures. I have charts from last week and operating reports to finish and file."

"Well, you can catch up on a bit of paperwork but you don't want to push yourself too hard."

She arched an eyebrow. "Well, I don't want to hold you back. If you have work at the hospital, go, I'll be fine."

"My orders were clear," he said.

"And you don't challenge your father?"

No. I don't.

Only he didn't say that. He kept his mouth shut.

"I'm to make sure you don't have a setback on the road to recovery," he said.

"So, paperwork day, then?" she asked. "That sounds good."

He could hear the displeasure in her voice, because he felt the same way about doing some of the niggly administrative stuff that he'd let build up. He preferred to be on the front lines patching people up. Saving lives.

And though he should let her just relax and do paperwork, he didn't want to do that either and he couldn't help when the next words came out of his mouth, "Eira had an interesting idea."

"Oh?" she asked, perking up.

"She knows my father all too well and that this is probably your only chance to have a couple of days off to play tourist."

"Are you offering to take me around and act as tour guide?" she asked, a sparkle of mischief in her eyes. One that made his pulse kick up a notch.

"If you'd like," he said off handedly.

"Okay, that sounds good. If you don't think that we'll get in trouble from your father."

"No, he won't know. He never leaves the hospital if he can help it."

The last time his father had taken time off was the day of his brother's funeral. Not that there had been a body to bury. Calder had been lost at sea.

He shook the image of the stone monument on the cliff outside town. The one that was the memorial for everyone who had died in that accident. Lost forever beneath the icy cold waves. All except him.

"You need to eat something first and then we can go." Axel spooned out some porridge for her and slid the bowl toward her. "Here."

"What is it?"

"*Hafragrautur*...or oatmeal, if you prefer." He slid some brown sugar over to her. "You can ease into it with this."

"It's thick!" she said, eyeing the bowl.

"It keeps the cold away."

"For a moment I thought you were serving me a bowl of grits."

"Grits? That sounds terrible. It sounds like dirt. What are grits?"

Betty chuckled as she spooned some brown sugar onto her porridge. "Instead of oats it's coarsely ground corn. It can be savory or sweet."

"That doesn't sound too bad."

"I haven't had grits in a long time," she said wistfully.

"You don't have grits in New York?"

"Not proper ones. It's a southern dish. I haven't had it since my grandmother died. She lived in southern Tennessee. Chattanooga."

"I don't know where that is," he said, chuckling.

"Well, I'm not too familiar with Iceland either. Other than the fact that you have volcanoes and black sand beaches."

"The beaches will be cold, and you can't get the sutures wet so the blue lagoon is out." He tapped his chin. "I think we'll just stick close and wander around Reykjavik if you don't mind."

"I don't mind at all. It sounds great. Just promise me one thing," she said.

"What's that?"

"Don't carry me around today. I don't want to experience Reykjavik hanging over your shoulder with my main view of the city being your butt." Her cheeks went red and she covered her mouth. Axel couldn't help but burst out laughing.

"Oh, my God, I'm so sorry. I didn't mean…"

"It's okay, Betty. It's okay and, no, I promise you I won't be carrying you around the city today. Eat your breakfast and we'll head out."

Axel left the kitchen, chuckling.

Today was going to be interesting.

* * *

Even though it had been bitter cold the last couple of days and there had been a snowstorm the night before, the temperatures were slightly milder as they walked toward the old town. Axel's home wasn't far from Hallgrímskirkja Church.

It was nice to get some exercise and some fresh air, but she still felt like a fool for the slip of the tongue. And it had to do with all those dreams she'd been having about Axel.

She could've sworn she had a dream that he came into her room last night and kissed her. The dream had been so real too. It was as if she could still feel his lips burned against hers, still feel his hands on her body. The dream had been so real.

She'd never had a dream like that before.

It was unnerving.

And then she had to go and talk about staring at his backside.

At least he thought it was funny.

Or it had appeared he thought it was funny at first. He'd certainly laughed enough and that was the first time she'd really seen him laugh. She'd liked it, but now as they were walking side by side he wasn't saying anything.

It was so tense. The only reason she knew he

was still walking beside her was the fact she could see his breath every once and a while out of her peripheral vision.

"So what's at Hallgrímskirkja?" she asked.

"It's an impressive cathedral. We might be able to climb to the top today, if it's open, but if not we can check out Leif Erikson's statue."

"Leif Erikson. I should probably know who he is."

Axel shot her a surprised look. "Everyone knows who Leif Erikson is. He was the first explorer to discover North America. He was son of Erik the Red. He was said to have founded L'Anse aux Meadows in Canada. And his father founded the first settlement in Greenland."

"So he's an important figure."

"He is." Axel nodded.

"And here I thought Christopher Columbus was the first to discover North America."

"No, Leif beat him." Axel grinned and winked at her and she felt completely at ease with him again.

"And after we pay homage to Leif?"

"Lunch in Old Town. Perhaps we'll have some of that beer I mentioned before."

"The Gold Viking?"

He chuckled softly. "Sure."

"I don't know. I'm sure your beer is stronger than beer in the States. I know Canadian beer is stronger than the US. And I'm not a beer drinker."

"We'll find you something."

"Well, you're the tour guide and I'm just the tourist."

"Exactly." Axel nodded.

"And you said this was Eira's idea?"

"It was."

"Remind me to thank her later."

Axel chuckled again. "She said I was wound too tight."

"She knows you well," Betty said offhandedly.

"What?" he asked, shocked.

"You didn't smile the first time I met you. You just complained about my footwear and then hoisted me over your shoulder and into your SUV."

And her blood heated as she recalled that first meeting. Watching that tall, broody Viking come marching across Keflavik airport as if he was on a mission. The way his hand had felt on her backside.

She usually didn't like alpha males. Thomas had taken charge in some aspects, but she couldn't picture Thomas parting a crowd and then literally sweeping her off her feet. No one had ever swept her off her feet as Axel had.

Of course, she'd never really been towered over by a man before. She was five feet nine. Axel was six feet two. Easily. She let her gaze wander over his body, just for a moment, until she could feel herself blushing again.

Get a grip.

It had to be the painkillers that were causing her to act like some kind of crazed woman. She had swooned over Thomas too, and look where that had gotten her.

A broken heart, shattered self-esteem and enough hurt to have her fleeing across the ocean to Iceland.

"There, you can see it now," Axel said, pointing.

As they started to climb a hill she got her first close-up look of Hallgrímskirkja, rising up into the sky.

"Whoa!"

There were tall churches in New York City like St. Patrick's, but those cathedrals were dwarfed by the rest of New York City's impressive skyline. Hallgrímskirkja sat out in the open, at the top of the hill overlooking the city.

It really was a sight to behold.

"It's great, isn't it?" Axel asked. "I do love

coming here. It's so strong. It just weathers everything and it stands so proudly."

"It really is impressive. I heard about it and caught glimpses of it, but it's really something to see standing up close."

"Let's go see if we can climb to the top." Axel took her hand and led her toward the church. It shocked her at first to feel her hand in his strong one, but she didn't mind.

"Do you really think climbing is smart for me?"

"Well, it's not a real climb. There's a lift and then a few steps to the viewing platform."

The tower and church were open. Axel paid the admission fee in the church shop, while Betty peeked inside the main cathedral of Hallgrímskirkja.

There was a large pipe organ. Probably the biggest she'd ever seen. Everything about the cathedral was awe-inspiring.

"Ready?" Axel asked.

"I'm ready. Though I will tell you now I'm afraid of heights, so if I freak out and don't get off the elevator you know why."

"You're afraid of heights?"

"Terrified. I've never been up the Empire State Building or the Statue of Liberty. I like to keep my feet firmly planted on the ground."

"I'll keep you safe." He took her hand again. "Come on."

There weren't very many tourists at Hall-grímskirkja, so they rode the elevator up to the top in privacy. The doors opened and her body tensed as she saw just how high they were above Reykjavik.

Her heart was going a mile a minute as her anxiety kicked in.

You're going to fall.

"Everything about you is so clenched," Axel teased. "It's okay."

"Is it?" Her eyes tracked a bird that flew by.

"It is." He held out his hand. "Come, I'll make sure you're safe."

She took a step forward. She was worried a gust of wind off the ocean would lift her up and toss her off Hallgrímskirkja, but surprisingly there was no wind in the sheltered top of the cathedral. It wasn't open to the air, there were windows and with that realization her body eased a bit.

"Come on." Axel led her to one of the windows and her body was shaking but he stood behind her, his arms around her, steadying her. His arms around her made her feel safe, but also extremely nervous. The last time a man had made her feel like this, well, she didn't want to think about it.

"What do you think of the view?"

"I don't know, I haven't looked yet," she said nervously, trying not to think about how his arms around her made her feel.

"Well, look," he said with a hint of amusement in his voice.

She opened her eyes and the first thing she saw was multicolored houses stretching out toward the sea.

"Wow, you can see all of the city from here."

"Yes. We're facing west, toward Greenland and North America."

"Too bad we can't see them from here."

"That would be impressive, but Greenland is about three hours by plane from here."

"Have you ever been there? Seeing how Leif Erikson's father was Erik the Red and he discovered Greenland?"

"And you said you didn't know anything about Leif Erikson."

"Well, not really," she teased. "I heard it from someone once."

Axel chuckled, "Well, to answer your question I have been to Greenland."

"What was it like?" she asked.

"Not green," he said dryly.

She laughed.

"You're not shaking any more," he whispered against her ear, which sent a zing of electricity down her spine.

"What're you talking about?"

"When I first put my arms around you, you were shaking like a leaf."

Warmth crept up into her cheeks. She didn't know how to respond to that. So she shrugged out of his arms and stepped away from the window toward the lift.

She had to put some distance between them if she wanted to keep their relationship professional and friendly.

"I'm hungry. Do you want to get some lunch? I'm feeling a bit dizzy."

"Sure. We can go get some lunch," Axel said.

Betty nodded. That tension that was there between them before was back and it was her fault it was back, but it was for the best.

She wasn't here for a relationship. She was here to work. To find herself and regain her confidence.

CHAPTER NINE

HE'D PUSHED TOO HARD.

And he knew better than that. He should've just kept his distance from her, but he couldn't help himself. When he was around her, everything else just melted away. He quickly forgot who he was now.

It just felt right.

You can't let it feel that way.

And he had to keep reminding himself to keep his distance. Betty was only here for a short time and by the way she moved away from him and changed the subject, by the way she couldn't even look him in the eye, he could tell that she had no interest in him.

She was playing it smart.

They were colleagues. They were friends and nothing more. The only way it could be.

And he had to remember that.

Axel owed it to his brother to devote his

life to Eira, to be there for her always. It was Calder who had thrown him out of the helicopter, saving Axel from the brunt of the blast.

Don't think about it.

And putting Eira first made dating nearly impossible. His last serious girlfriend had wanted nothing to do with the responsibility of caring for a child. She'd left him and it had made him realize he was better off going it alone.

He glanced over at Betty, who was staring up at the ceiling of the lift. She wasn't making eye contact with him and he hated himself for stepping out of bounds with her. It was just, she was so beautiful. So kind, so funny.

Betty was clumsy and quirky.

It was a change.

The lift stopped and the doors slid open. Axel held the door back to allow Betty to get off and then he slipped out, letting other people get on.

Now there was a small crowd going up to the observation tower of the cathedral. He was glad they had gone up when they had and had the viewing tower all to themselves for that one stolen moment, allowing Axel to forget about who he had become.

He wasn't in the tactical navy any longer. He

wasn't out on the water or in the sky, things that he used to love more than anything.

He was caged.

Under his father's thumb, but that was fitting punishment for surviving when Calder hadn't.

"You okay?" Betty asked as they walked out of the cathedral, meandering back toward the statue of Leif Eriksson.

"Fine."

But he wasn't fine.

He was just good at hiding it. "Where do you want to eat?" he asked, changing the subject.

She shrugged, her hands in her pockets. "I wouldn't even know where to begin. You're the tour guide for the day."

He smiled gently. "I did say that, didn't I?"

Betty nodded. "I'll leave the choice up to you, then."

"Old town it is."

As they were heading down the hill there was a commotion behind him and then a scream, which sent a chill down his spine.

They both spun around and he saw a man collapsed on the ground at the crest of the hill, near the statue where he and Betty had been moments before. Axel went running and he could hear Betty behind him.

He was down on his knees beside the man who was convulsing on the ground.

"What happened?" he asked the woman who had cried out.

"I don't know. One minute we were talking about going up the tower of the cathedral, the next thing he told me the heartburn he'd been having was really bothering him and suddenly he was on the ground. Are you a doctor?"

"I am," Axel said. "Have you called the paramedics?"

"Yes," the woman said.

Betty was kneeling beside him, holding the man as Axel pulled off his jacket and placed it over him.

Axel checked the man's pupils and airway, making a precursory evaluation. All the while in his head he was going through the symptoms, trying to figure out what could be the cause.

"What did she say? I couldn't understand what she was saying," Betty whispered.

"He was having bad heartburn."

The wail of a siren grew louder as the ambulance came up the hill and parked on the green, bringing a stretcher.

"Dr. Sturlusson." The young paramedic who

had dealt with Betty the night of the accident was there. "What do we have?"

"The patient collapsed after complaining of significant heartburn. He has a laceration from where his head hit the cement. His pulse rate is sixty and his pupils are equal and reactive."

The paramedic nodded and they worked together to get the man up onto the stretcher and hooked up to an IV for fluids and a cannula for oxygen.

As they loaded the patient into the ambulance the young paramedic turned to them. "Can I assume you're taking him once we get to the hospital?"

Axel should tell him no, that he wasn't working today, but this was his patient and he wanted to see it through.

He always saw his patients through.

"I'll be there. Let the emergency room staff know Dr. Jacinth and I will be taking this patient."

The young paramedic nodded and Axel turned back to Betty.

"Care to take a rain check on lunch and go to the hospital to possibly repair an aortic aneurysm?"

"Isn't that for a cardiothoracic surgeon?"

"You're looking at a fully qualified surgeon,

who happens to also specialize in trauma. I can do it. I've done it before in emergency situations. I can handle this."

Betty's eyebrows arched. "Color me impressed."

"Let's go."

"Right behind you."

Axel hailed a cab and soon the taxi was whisking them off to the hospital. They arrived just after the ambulance had pulled up and was unloading the patient.

As the stretcher hit the ground Axel had his hands on it, wheeling his patient through the doors and ordering instructions to the flurry of residents who were there to meet the ambulance.

Betty was on the other side, calling for her scrubs and ordering tests for a possible rupture aortic aneurysm.

The paramedics signed off on the patient and one of the residents filled in the patient's distraught wife on what was happening.

Once Axel had the tests ordered and the patient was in the capable hands of the surgical residents Axel and Betty headed to the locker room to change. As Axel rounded the corner, his father came out of an exam room.

"Axel and Dr. Jacinth, what're you both

doing here?" he asked. "You're supposed to be taking it easy, Dr. Jacinth."

"I'm fine—" Betty started to explain, but Axel cut her off.

"A patient collapsed at the cathedral. He's my patient and I'm the one who was first on scene. I will be the one taking care of him and since I'm supposed to be watching Dr. Jacinth, she's going to be assisting me."

His father was clearly stunned, but couldn't really argue back because Betty was standing there. And he knew that his father didn't want to make a bad impression on Betty. Instead his father stepped to the side, but Axel knew that this wasn't the end of it.

He knew that once the patient was stable his father would be calling him on the carpet for disobeying his orders but Axel would deal with that later. Right now, he was going to focus on saving this man's life.

Betty followed him into the locker room and they began to peel off their street clothes and slip their scrubs on. Axel tried not to watch as she changed in front of him, but he couldn't help but notice her.

As if she knew he was assessing her she turned and looked at him as she tied up her sneakers. She smiled at him.

"Are you sure you're up for this?" he asked, shutting his locker. "I didn't mean to strong-arm you into doing a surgery if you're not fully recovered."

"I'm fine, Axel. I don't have a concussion and I don't think anyone has strong-armed me into doing a surgery before."

Axel chuckled. "I just wanted to make sure you were up for this."

"I'm up for this."

"Our outings always seem to end on a note of disaster," he remarked. It was something of a weird occurrence, forcing them to work together, and he didn't mind. He liked working with Betty.

"That they do." She walked over to him and clapped him on the shoulder. "Let's go save a life."

Axel finished getting ready and they both headed out onto the trauma floor.

"Dr. Sturlusson, I have the CT scans of Mr. Bjorn."

"Thank you, Dr. Einnarsson." Axel took the scans from the resident and could see where the aorta had torn away from the heart. "Dr. Einnarsson, can you prep the patient and have an intern prep an operating theatre for an emergency aortic dissection?"

"Yes, Dr. Sturlusson." The resident walked away quickly.

"I guess we'd better get ready for surgery," Betty said. "I'll go make sure the operating theatre is prepped and write it on the board."

Axel nodded. "Make sure that Dr. Einnarsson is the resident who is assisting."

Betty nodded and walked toward the operating-room floor.

Axel found the patient's wife pacing just outside the emergency-room doors. He took a deep breath and went out to inform the poor woman that her life was about to change.

And to prepare herself for the worst.

"Suction, please," Axel stated calmly as he worked to remove the damaged portions of the man's torn aorta. The next step would be repairing it with a graft while the patient was on bypass and, by the looks of the dissection, he would have to repair the valve on Mr. Bjorn's heart from where the tear started.

After talking with the patient's wife, Axel learned that Mr. Bjorn, who was a Swedish tourist, had suffered from problems with high blood pressure. He fit the usual demographic of such a dissection. Middle age, high-blood-pressure problems. The poor man thought he was just having heartburn, when really he was experiencing something far more sinister.

Axel glanced up to see Betty across the table from him.

Just like before when he'd been in the operating room with her while she was doing an emergency cholecystectomy, they were working together so well. It was as if she'd been his partner his whole surgical career.

It was a nice change.

He usually avoided working with other surgeons or doing a vast majority of the cardiothoracic surgeries. His father liked to remind him over and over that Axel didn't have seniority here. Just because he'd served on the tactical navy, just because he'd saved lives every day for those lost and injured at sea, just because he was an excellent cardiothoracic surgeon and trauma surgeon, didn't give him first choice of what surgeries he did.

And as he was the son of the Chief of Surgery, other surgeons thought he was either a spy for his father or spoiled. Axel preferred to work alone anyways. He was controlling about how he did things, because how he did things saved lives. He didn't have time to explain his process to others.

Working with Betty was completely different. She understood him.

"You're doing a fine job on that repair, Dr. Sturlusson," Betty said, her hands working beside his as they did the repair together.

"As are you, Dr. Jacinth." Axel looked around and could see surgical interns hovering in the background. As well as the resident, Dr. Einnarsson, who was standing next to Betty. There was something else he never really got to do either and that was teach while he did his surgery. Also, he never really drew a crowd like this.

"Dr. Einnarsson, can you tell me what the protocol will be for our patient here once he is discharged?"

Dr. Einnarsson's eyes opened wide above the surgical mask. "He will have follow-up scans and take blood-pressure medicine to treat his condition."

"Very good, because left unchecked his high blood pressure can rupture the graft." Axel finished removing the damaged section. "He'll be staying in Iceland for a while, to recover and make sure that his blood pressure is under control before it's safe to fly."

His pulse kicked up a notch as he thought about flying. He closed his eyes and counted back from ten and that little bit of anxiety that had flared at the thought of flying again faded.

Betty was watching him and her big blue eyes were wide with concern. As if she saw his small, momentary lapse of concentration.

"Dr. Jacinth, is everything okay?" Axel asked, not looking at her.

"Everything is great here, Dr. Sturlusson." That statement was laced with a question on the end. As if she was asking if everything was okay with him. As if she didn't believe him.

This is what happens when you let people get too close to you.

He should know better.

Once this surgery was done and Mr. Bjorn was in the ICU he was going to take Betty home, but not to his house. It was obvious that she was okay now so he was going to take her back to her rental.

Axel needed space.

He had to distance himself from Betty and that was hard to do when she was staying in the guest room. If he didn't distance himself now, then he would regret it. She would regret it too and he didn't want to hurt her.

There was no future for them together.

He didn't deserve someone like her.

* * *

Something had changed in that operating room. Betty wasn't sure what it was, but something about Axel had shifted and he had thrown up his walls again. Standing across from her as they finished repairing Mr. Bjorn's aortic dissection was that big, broody, annoying Viking who complained about her boots and then threw her over his shoulder like a marauder.

He wasn't the same Axel who had had his arms around her in the viewing tower of the cathedral. The one who'd spoken gently to her, carried her to bed, made her breakfast and smelled so good.

Yeah, he smelled really good.

When he'd been behind her, his arms on either side of her and his chest against her back, his head over her shoulder as he'd whispered in her ear, he'd smelled like sea and earth. Clean and masculine. And just thinking about his whispers in her ear made the butterflies in her stomach flutter.

And she was completely annoyed at herself for having that kind of reaction to him.

You are not here to fall for a man. You are not here to fall for a man.

She had to get some distance and the only

way she was going to get distance was if she returned to her rental. It would be a very bad idea to stay a couple more nights in Axel's house.

Axel came into the locker room and barely glanced at her.

"How is the patient?" she asked.

"He's stable and in the intensive care unit. His prognosis is good. I'm going to stay the night here though. I want to watch him."

"Okay. I was going to go back to my rental tonight, but if you want me to stay with Eira I can."

"Yeah, that would be great, and then I could help you move back to your place in the morning."

"That sounds good."

She was relieved and she was exhausted. Even though she didn't have a concussion, she was feeling the effects of her accident and lack of sleep right now, because of standing during the long, long surgery to repair Mr. Bjorn's aortic dissection.

"Thank you for helping me in there," he said. "I appreciate it."

"That's what I'm here to do."

He nodded, but still wouldn't really look her in the eye. "I'll see you tomorrow morning."

Axel left the locker room and Betty sat down on the bench and let out a sigh, running her hands through her hair.

Why did she have to muck up every relationship?

Her phone buzzed and she looked at it.

It was Thomas again.

And even though she knew she shouldn't answer it, she did.

"Thomas," she said with exasperation.

"Betty, I was beginning to think you'd fallen off the edge of the earth."

"You knew where I was, Thomas. I told you about the job when I accepted and gave you my sabbatical notice."

"Iceland is the edge of the earth."

"Not really. It's between North America and Europe."

Thomas sighed in exasperation on the other end of the phone. "I didn't call to argue over semantics with you."

"Then why did you call, Thomas? Aren't you supposed to be on your honeymoon?" Her stomach flip-flopped when she said that out loud.

"I am calling from Mexico."

She closed her eyes and could feel tears of

anger stinging her eyes. "Thomas, why are you calling me?"

"I need you," he whispered.

"Why are you whispering?"

Then she realized why Thomas started talking to her so weirdly. He wasn't alone. *She* was with him.

"Goodbye, Thomas." She disconnected the call and rubbed her eyes. She wouldn't cry. She wouldn't let him get under her skin again. That was why she'd come here. To put him behind her. But how could she do that when he was calling her and messaging her?

She wasn't sure if she could ever be free from him.

She got out of her scrubs and put on her street clothes. As she picked up her jeans her ticket for the cathedral slipped out of her pocket. She picked it up.

Their day had been so lovely.

Of course, when she'd gone out with Thomas that first time it had been magical too, for a short while. And then it had fallen apart. So horribly.

Tonight she'd stay with Eira and then she would go back to her own place and return to treating Axel as a regular work colleague.

She'd focus on putting the ghost of what

she'd had with Thomas to rest, then she would
be able to return to New York and move on
with her life. And she wanted so desperately
to move on. If only she could find the strength
to do just that.

She couldn't remember that last time she'd
felt strong. Coping with her father's death had
used up every ounce of strength she'd had. It
was hard to recall how she'd been before she'd
lost him. Before she met Thomas. That was
part of the problem too. She really didn't know
who she was any more. Betty glanced at the
receipt for the viewing tower. She crumpled
it up and threw it in a nearby trash can. She
finished getting dressed and headed out of the
locker room.

"Dr. Jacinth!"

Betty turned around and a young, handsome
man was waving at her, as if he knew her. He
was vaguely familiar.

"Can I help you?" she asked.

"I'm Stellan, I was the paramedic on the
night of the accident and at the cathedral." He
had really light blue eyes and blond hair and,
though he was undoubtedly handsome, he
didn't really hold a candle to Axel.

Don't think about him.

"Oh, yes I do remember you. Sorry, I'm not the best with faces sometimes."

He grinned at her, those blue eyes sparkling. "I was wondering how the patient with the aortic dissection was doing? Sometimes as a paramedic we don't really get to see the outcome of our cases."

"We repaired the dissection and the patient made it through surgery and is in the intensive care unit."

"Good," Stellan said, but he rubbed the back of his neck, as if he wanted to say more to her.

"Was that all?" Betty asked.

"No, I actually wanted to know if you wanted to go out for a drink?"

The question stunned her. "Actually, I'm watching a friend's niece tonight. Maybe another night?"

Stellan was disappointed. "Sure. Do you need a ride?"

"I can take a cab."

"No, I insist. It'll have to be in the ambulance as I need to return it to the depot, but I can take you home."

Betty was so tired and she didn't want to leave Eira alone for any longer so she found the address in her text messages because she wasn't sure she could properly pronounce the street name without Stellan laughing at her. "Do you know where this is?"

Stellan leaned over her phone. "I know exactly where that is. It's not far from my place. Let's go."

Betty was relieved. She followed Stellan out to the ambulance, but had a feeling that someone was watching her. She turned around briefly, but no one was there.

CHAPTER TEN

FOR THE LAST WEEK, since the day he'd taken her back to her rental after the accident, Axel had managed to avoid Betty. He'd been able to largely avoid his father as well, with the notable exception of their confrontation after the surgery when the old man had lit into him about bringing Betty back to work against his wishes.

But Betty was clearly fine, her laceration was on the mend and she hadn't had a concussion. She was running the surgical resident program and working with the residents well.

Better than he ever had.

And his father was clearly happy that she was doing so well.

His father had remarked that Betty was a chip off the old block, just as talented as her late father had been.

Mr. Bjorn was on the mend and Axel was

overseeing his care. It was good enough for Axel. He was able to melt back into the background and just do his work. Even though it was hard to keep his distance from Betty. He missed her and it was difficult having to see that paramedic, Stellan, showing his interest her.

The night that Betty had watched Eira, he'd seen Stellan and Betty leave the hospital together. He'd seen the way she smiled when she talked to Stellan. Knew that Stellan had a bigger personality. He was charming and several doctors in the hospital spoke highly of him.

It was no wonder that he seemed to be sweeping Betty off her feet.

Stellan could offer her more than he could.

Axel was tied to Iceland and Stellan probably didn't have the same ties as Axel did.

Betty deserved to have someone who could make her smile, the way she smiled when she was around Stellan.

Axel scrubbed his hand over his face and took another sip of his now cold coffee. He'd been working at catching up on his charts for several hours, but he wasn't getting far. Not when his mind kept wandering.

Eira had been so displeased with him when he'd returned home only to take Betty back to her place. She was angry that he'd sent Betty away. She didn't understand why he wasn't trying and Axel didn't have the capacity to explain to her why he wasn't trying.

Why he didn't deserve a chance. If he explained it, it would just bring back all those painful memories for Eira. Getting Eira to this point, where she was opening up and becoming a bit more mature, was a step forward. He didn't need to take a step back and he didn't want to open old wounds with her.

So he gladly bore the cold shoulder at home.

He closed his eyes.

"You okay?"

He opened his eyes to see Betty standing on the other side of the nursing station where he'd been working.

"Tired," he said quickly.

"I haven't seen you around."

"You've been busy with the residents, doing the job you were brought here to do, and I've been busy with patients."

She smiled warmly at him. "I know, but you looked—"

"How did I look?" Axel snapped. "I'm tired. Nothing more."

"Fine. You're tired. I'm sorry for asking, I thought we were friends and I had a feeling you were avoiding me. I guess I wasn't wrong about that."

"What makes you think I'm avoiding you?"

"For one thing, you didn't offer to carry me up to my house when you dropped me off." There was a twinkle of humor in her eyes and he couldn't help but crack a smile.

"You made it to the top of the cathedral despite your fear of heights. I think you're now capable of safely walking the icy Reykjavik streets."

She cocked an eyebrow. "Are you referring to me as a street walker?"

"Does that mean something else in America?"

"It's a colloquial term for prostitute."

Good job.

"I'm sorry," he said, chuckling a bit. "That's not what I meant at all."

"I know. How's Eira?"

"She's fine," he answered tightly.

"Oh, that bad, huh?"

"She's mad that you left and that I didn't make you stay. She thinks it's as bad as me kicking you out."

"Do you want me to have a talk with her?" Betty asked.

"No, it's fine. She'll get over it. I just think…"

He trailed off because he didn't want to tell Betty what he thought, that Eira was trying to reclaim some kind of semblance of happy family. Calder and their mother were the two in the family who always knew how to make a house feel like a home. They were the glue that held the family together.

Axel and his father, they just couldn't seem to make a connection. To keep that sense of family. To make a house a home.

Calder always said Axel and their father were the same. Axel didn't see it, because he was trying and his father wasn't.

"I get it," Betty said. There was a flush of pink in her cheek. "Well, I'll let you get back to work."

He felt so bad for brushing her off.

What was wrong with him?

"Betty, wait."

She turned around.

"I wouldn't mind if you talk to Eira. I think she needs a woman's input."

Betty's expression softened. "Okay. I can do that."

Axel sank down in his seat and finished the rest of his cold coffee. Angry at himself for everything he had done wrong.

He was a surgeon. Mechanical and cold-hearted.

And he would never be anything else. Calder had been right. He was just like his father.

Axel finished the rest of his surgical and post-operative notes. It took him most of the day because he would often get interrupted by residents who were working the trauma floor, especially if Betty was busy with another patient. But he didn't mind.

He also made several visits to check on Mr. Bjorn and monitor his blood pressure. He was glad to see that his patient was taking to the blood-pressure-medicine protocol well.

"You saved his life," Mrs. Bjorn said as Axel finished checking the incision sight and changing the bandage.

"He's got a strong will to live," Axel said, not taking the compliment.

"But you were there. If you weren't there he…" Mrs. Bjorn looked away, brushing the tears from her eyes.

He wanted to tell her that even if he hadn't been there, paramedics still would've come and someone else here would've done the surgery.

"Well, I'm glad I was there that day too."

Mr. Bjorn smiled weakly at him, in thanks.

"Do you know when we'll be able to go home?" she asked.

"Not for some time. I want to make sure he's fully healed and that he'll be able to take the cabin-pressure changes on the flight. He's also at a risk for a pulmonary embolus. I promise you, Mrs. Bjorn, we're doing all we can to get you both home safely and healthy as quickly as possible. I have contacted your family physician in Sweden. He's up to date on everything and once we get your husband strong enough to travel, I'm confident your family doctor can take it from there."

"Oh, good," Mrs. Bjorn said in relief.

Axel pulled off the rubber gloves and disposed of everything. He cleaned his hands with hand sanitizer and then left the room. As soon as he stepped out of the door his phone went off. Eira was texting him.

She wanted to meet for dinner in Old Town. She wanted to talk to him.

Axel responded that he'd be there at seven. He slipped his phone into his pocket and then ran smack dab into the last person he wanted to see.

His father.

His father appeared flustered and annoyed.

"How is your aortic dissection patient progressing?"

"He's doing well," Axel said.

"And your delinquent post-operative reports?"

"All done. Have you reconsidered my request to join the cardiothoracic team now? I want to learn more under the head of Cardio. He is more than willing to take me on. I've learned the basics as a trauma surgeon."

"Why would I do that? You're a trauma doctor."

Axel's jaw clenched. Of course. His father was never going to see him for who he was. He didn't even know why he was bothering to try. His father was going to hold him back and keep him down just to keep punishing him.

"This is me trying to improve, Father."

"You're a trauma doctor. I don't need you on the cardio team."

"Of course. Well, if you'll excuse me, I have to finish my rounds and then I'm meeting Eira for dinner. You could join us, if you'd like?"

"What?" his father asked, as if he'd been slapped.

"Your granddaughter. When was the last time you saw her, Father?"

"I see her during the holidays," his father snapped.

"You can see her more than that. I know she would like it."

"Don't speak to me about Eira," his father said under his breath. "You have no right to talk to me about her."

"I only thought that you might like to have dinner with us. That's all."

"I'm busy," his father said, nodding curtly before storming away.

Axel shook his head. He wished Calder and his mother were here. They would be able to reach out to his father and help them bridge the gap. His mother had had a way of softening their father; without her his father just lived in this perpetual cloud of anger and bitterness.

Aren't you doing just the same?

Axel shook that thought away. He didn't have time to think about this. He had his rounds to finish and then he'd meet Eira for dinner. Maybe they could talk about what had happened with Betty. Maybe *he* could be the one to try to bridge the gap, but he was afraid he just didn't know how.

"Betty, I'm so glad I found you."

Betty looked up from where she was going

over a chart to see Eira standing in front of her. The girl had a big smile on her face and looked a lot better than she had when they'd first met.

"Eira, what're you doing here?"

"Well, I'm here to get my stitches out." Eira held up her arm. "It's been two weeks."

Betty smiled. "Of course. Let's get you settled into an exam room."

"Great."

Eira fell into step beside Betty. They found an empty exam room and Eira set her stuff down in one of the chairs before climbing up into the larger chair that was used for triage, blood work and assessments of patients.

Betty found what she needed to remove the sutures in the cupboards.

"I thought you would've gone to your family doctor or had your uncle remove the stitches," Betty said as she set down all the things she would need to do the job.

"No, I wanted you to do them. I hope you don't mind?"

"Not at all." Betty pulled on a pair of rubber gloves and dabbed alcohol on a cotton ball before cleaning the incision.

Eira winced. "That's cold."

"This won't hurt very much or for very long."

Betty examined the healed wound, glad to see all signs of infection were gone.

"Are you sure?" Eira asked nervously.

"Positive. I got stitches in my leg when I was about your age and I had a lot more than you have here. I was so worried that it was going to hurt, but it was fine. The sensation was a bit weird, but, really, it doesn't hurt much at all."

"Okay." Eira closed her eyes and Betty could see that her other hand was clenched.

"Relax, it's going to be all right."

Betty started to do her work and it didn't take long before the stitches were out and she was cleaning up the remnants.

"Is it over?" Eira asked in surprise.

"It is." Betty disposed of everything and placed the surgical instruments in a bucket to be sent off to be sterilized.

"Oh, I'm so glad and you're right—it didn't hurt."

"See, I told you."

Eira bit her lip and Betty instantly suspected there was something else she wanted to say to her, but it was clear the younger girl was nervous.

"Eira, you know that you can talk to me if you need to. Your uncle doesn't mind us talking."

She looked relieved. "Well, I was actually

hoping that we could go out for dinner and talk about something that's bothering me."

"Sure. When were you thinking?"

"Are you available now?"

Betty glanced at her watch. It was almost six-thirty and her shift was supposed to be over at five-thirty.

"Yeah, I'm done for the night. I'll just change and we can walk into Old Town together?"

Eira nodded, grinning. "Yes and I know a perfect place."

"Sounds great."

Betty changed quickly and then returned to the emergency room to find Eira loitering around the nurses' station. Eira appeared nervous, almost jumpy, looking around as if she was afraid that her uncle or possibly her grandfather was going to see her.

Maybe Axel really isn't okay with it.

And if Axel wasn't okay with it, she shouldn't go.

Eira turned and smiled at Betty. "Are you ready?"

"Eira, are you sure your uncle is okay with this? I mean, he told me that he was okay if you turned to me to talk but…"

"But what? If he said it's okay, then it's fine."

"You look like you're ready to bolt," Betty

teased as she slipped on her winter jacket and wound her infinity scarf around her neck.

"I don't want to run into my grandfather," Eira admitted sheepishly. "He doesn't like children lingering in his emergency room."

Betty was stunned. "Oh, okay, well, let's go so that he doesn't get the chance to get angry with you for being here."

Eira smiled and nodded.

They chatted about weather and school as they took the short walk through lightly falling snow to Old Town, Eira leading them toward a cozy café that was in an older building just off the main street.

Inside it was all wood and stone, with a roaring fireplace in the center. They found a booth near the back and Eira ordered a couple of coffees for them.

"Usually fourteen-year-olds don't drink coffee."

Eira looked at her in disbelief. "I find that hard to believe. Besides, I'll be fifteen soon and most of us drink coffee. Or at least in my circle of friends."

Betty tried not to laugh. Eira was so cute. There were flashes of confidence, though they were rare, but that confidence completely suited her.

"So what did you want to talk about?" Betty asked, folding her hands on the table in front of her.

Eira smiled at her hands. "I feel like I'm in an interview."

"You're not." Betty chuckled. "Sorry, it's just usually how I sit. I don't have many dinners that are not business related."

"You live in New York City and you're a young, single woman. Shouldn't you be out there dating? Like on all the American TV shows set in New York City."

Betty's mouth dropped open and now she was embarrassed. "A surgeon doesn't have much time for dating. And what're you doing watching those shows?"

Eira ignored her question. "I guess that's why doctors marry other doctors. Their dating pool is very small."

"Was your mother a doctor?" Betty asked gently. She didn't want to bring up a topic that might be sore for Eira, but Eira wanted to speak to her about something that was obviously bothering her.

"She was a nurse practitioner for the tactical navy," Eira said. There was no hint of sadness in her voice, just pride. "She died of cancer."

"She had cancer when she was pregnant with you?" Betty asked, shocked.

"She did. She refused treatment. I always used to worry that my father resented me, but then…" Eira trailed off. There were tears in her eyes. "He loved me. And he made sure that I knew how much my mother loved me."

"And how about your uncle?" Betty asked.

"He loves me." Eira smiled brightly at her. "He just…he blames himself for my father's death. I don't think that he thinks he's good enough and he pushes people away."

Betty knew that feeling all too well. Thomas had made her feel not good enough so many times and every time she tried to find her confidence again, he was right there, pulling her back into the toxic cycle of their relationship and she let him. Why did she let him?

"He didn't mean to send you away, Betty," Eira said quickly, interrupting Betty's train of thought.

"He didn't send me away, Eira. I didn't have a concussion. I was cleared to work so he took me back to my place. I wasn't supposed to move in with you."

"But what if you did?" Eira asked.

"Eira, I don't think…" Betty trailed off as

she saw a familiar figure move through the crowded little bistro toward the back booth.

Axel.

Her heart skipped a beat and she was suddenly very nervous. Their gazes locked and his expression was unreadable, but she could tell by the way his posture straightened that he wasn't too pleased to see her.

"Betty," he said curtly, nodding, and then he turned to Eira. "I thought it was going to be just us tonight?"

Eira grinned and blushed. "I thought that you two had a bit of a falling-out and I wanted to make things right."

"Eira, we didn't have a falling out," Betty said.

Only they had.

They had both put up walls after that aortic dissection surgery a week ago.

And apparently they weren't the only ones who saw this.

"Uncle Axel, you need to enjoy life and I know that you two get along so well. It was so nice when Betty was around and I think you both miss each other."

Betty was completely stunned and Axel said nothing.

"My friends are waiting for me," Eira said

brightly, nodding toward a group of teenage girls standing by the door, and then slipping out of the booth. She stood on her tiptoes and kissed her uncle on the cheek. "I'm going over to Janetje's tonight. Please, you two, just talk. For me?"

Betty was too stunned to say anything else.

Axel didn't say anything as he watched his niece disappear off with a couple of girlfriends. He stood there for a few minutes more and then slipped into the booth across from Betty.

"I'm sorry," he said, clearing his throat.

"For what?" she asked, still stunned by Eira's manipulation of them both.

"For Eira." A small smile tugged at the corner of his mouth. "She was always pushy when she was young. She always wanted to get her way and my brother would usually let her get away with murder."

She laughed. "I can see that. She's a very charming young woman."

The waitress came and set down the coffee and looked confused by the change in occupants to the booth. "Will this be all?"

Betty looked at Axel. "I can go for a bite to eat. What about you?"

He didn't say anything and for a moment she thought he was going to get up and leave.

"I can definitely eat." He turned to the waitress and ordered some food.

When the waitress left Betty leaned over the table. "What did you just order for us?"

Axel chuckled and there was that twinkle in his eyes again. "*Hangikjöt*. It's lamb. It's quite tasty."

"Okay, well, if it's not I'm totally blaming you."

He smiled. It was rare to see him smile so brightly, and she enjoyed the reappearance of the delicious dimples he had, which she just wanted to eat up. Axel was the most handsome man she'd ever seen, but it wasn't just his physical looks. There was something about Axel that made her weak in the knees.

Something that made her forget that he was totally off limits.

"That's all right. You know, I should've known Eira would pull something like this. As I told you before, she was angry when you left our house."

"I thought she was being jumpy in the emergency room because she didn't want her grandfather to catch her loitering, but it's obvious now that she was on the lookout for you."

Axel's smile disappeared. "It was probably a combination of both. My father doesn't like children hanging out in the hospital. With patients it's fine, but physicians' and nurses' children should be at home in his opinion. He's always enforced that. And, unfortunately, Eira and I have borne the brunt of his lectures. No visiting at the workplace. At all."

"I'm sorry to hear that. Your father is just so nice to me and—"

"He respected your father," Axel said, gently cutting her off. "But when my brother Calder first died, Eira was afraid of losing any more of her family so I brought her to work with me one day. She had been crying and clinging to me, frightened. I only had to stop at the hospital to do a quick consult and I saw no problem bringing her. My father felt otherwise."

Betty's heart sank. "I'm sorry to hear that. It's usually not a problem anywhere else."

"I've tried to get my father more interested in Eira, but he's not the best with children."

"Or you," Betty said quickly and Axel shot her a look that made her instantly regret what she'd said.

"You're not wrong there," Axel said, sighing. "My father and I never had the best relationship when I was younger, but when my mother died and then my brother the following year, our relationship combusted."

"He's grieving. People grieve in very different ways. I threw myself into a destructive relationship that I can't seem to escape from when my father died."

Axel cocked his head to one side. "With Thomas Welling?"

"Yes. My father told me, right before he died and when I started my surgical residency, to not get involved with another doctor until I was established. He told me to focus on becoming the best damn surgeon I could be. After my internship, he passed away so suddenly and it destroyed my world. It was an aortic dissection and the best team of cardiothoracic surgeons were right at his doorstep at Mayo, but he was in his office, working, and he died before they could find him."

"I'm sorry to hear that."

"Thanks."

"And so when did you start seeing Thomas?"

"About a year after the funeral. I was done with my first year of residency and I was a promising general surgeon. I was the 'one to watch' and then Thomas walked into my life and I let him walk all over me. He got all the accolades for our work. Suddenly, I wasn't the one to watch, he was, but I didn't care because I was in love."

"I understand that. My last relationship also ended in heartbreak."

"Oh?" Betty asked, just slightly jealous. Although she shouldn't be surprised—a handsome, caring, strong man like Axel wouldn't be single for long.

"Freya and I were together for three years and then after my brother died and I had to take care of Eira she was angry. She felt my father should take care of Eira, and she wasn't completely thrilled about my post-traumatic stress or my grief. So she left. She said it wasn't fair for me to expect her to bear that burden."

"Wow. She sounds like a real piece of work."

Axel chuckled. "And your Thomas sounds like a right jerk."

"He was. I let him control my life for far too long. So long that I faded into the background and every time I tried to move forward, he reeled me back in. So that's why I'm here. In Reykjavik. About to eat…hangikjöt?"

Axel chuckled. "Yes and that is the correct pronunciation."

"At least I'm learning something."

"You're still one to watch." His eyes were so intense, so serious, and it made her heart beat a bit faster. The compliment caught her off guard. She could feel the heat blooming in her cheeks.

She didn't know how to respond to that and luckily she didn't have to as the waitress chose that moment to bring them their food.

Betty appreciated the compliment, even if it wasn't really true.

She wasn't one to watch.

She didn't want to be watched. She just wanted to disappear for a while. To mend herself so that maybe then she could move on with her life.

Axel couldn't believe that Eira had been so devious and had set this up. This reminded him of the mischievous things his brother used to do. At first he'd thought about walking away and not sitting down to have dinner, but he couldn't hurt Betty like that.

And he missed her.

There was still pink in her cheeks from his comment that she was still one to watch. She looked embarrassed, but not flattered as he'd hoped.

"I didn't mean to make you uncomfortable, Betty," he said gently, and he reached out and took her hand. "I'm sorry I've been being such a…"

"Doofus," Betty mumbled.

"What's a doofus?"

"A jerk."

He chuckled. "Yeah, that. I'm sorry, I just thought it might be better for your reputation at the hospital if you weren't associated with me so I've kept my distance. I'm the black sheep. They either see me as a threat because I'm the son of Dr. Sturla Sturlusson and resent me, or they feel pity for me because they know about Calder. Either way, I'm not well liked at the hospital."

"I'm sorry that they're so jealous," Betty said, squeezing his hand back. "You are talented, but I do have one question."

"Sure."

"Can you explain the surname thing to me? Your father is Sturla Sturlusson. I knew he was S. Sturlusson, but Sturla?"

Axel grinned. "His father was Sturla as well. That is how last names are derived. The last name forms the father's name. My mother thought there should be a break in the name and called me Axel and my brother Calder. So Eira is actually Calderdóttir, because she is a female. My sons will be Axelsson and my daughters Axeldóttir."

"In the States we just take on our parents'

surnames. Jacinth is French, or something. My father never knew. Whoever they were, they settled in Tennessee."

"Do you miss home?"

She cocked her head to one side. "No, since my father died and my grandmother before him, I don't really have a place to call home. I do miss New York, sometimes, but I didn't really do much outside the hospital after…"

He could tell she was thinking about Thomas and he felt bad.

"Don't think about him," Axel said gently.

"I'm not thinking about him," she said stiffly.

"Let's talk about something else. Why did you want to go into trauma and laparoscopic surgery?"

"Why did you want to do trauma and cardiothoracic?" she asked, turning the table on him.

"I asked you first!" he teased.

She smiled, those beautiful eyes of hers twinkling. "I just liked the fast pace of the emergency room, but I do like doing laparoscopic surgeries, when I need a break from the gritty world of the trauma room. It's a delicate surgery, slow and methodical. Less invasive compared to trauma. Now it's your turn."

"I wanted to be a cardiothoracic surgeon

since I left medical school, but my brother joined the tactical navy as a surgeon and I idolized my brother. So I joined too. I learned everything I could and was able to work with an amazing cardiothoracic surgeon out in the field. If I had my choice I would be doing cardiothoracic work every day. There's a beauty to the heart. Not many people can see that."

"Why didn't you take a job on the cardiothoracic team, then, after your time in the tactical navy?"

"Because my father is punishing me." He couldn't believe he'd admitted to it.

"He's punishing you?"

"When the helicopter started to go down, there was an explosion and my brother grabbed me and threw me into the water first. He took the blast of shrapnel to his back. He was injured, probably paralyzed and he died. And I came out of it unscathed. Calder was my father's favorite. Calder could calm him, much like my mother could. My father blamed me for living instead of Calder, so, he's punishing me."

"Are you sure?"

"He told me so," Axel said.

"That's cruel," she said gently.

"He's only this way with me and Eira, if I'm

honest. Eira reminds him of my mother and of Calder. So he pushes her away."

"He's afraid to let her in because he might lose her, perhaps?"

Axel nodded. "So am I. I promised my brother I would watch her. That I would take care of her. I don't feel like I'm doing good enough for her."

"You are," Betty said and she touched his hand again. "You really are."

He wanted to take her hand and kiss it, but the waitress came over to their table and placed the beer he'd ordered in front of them.

"You ordered beer?"

"Who said I did?" he teased.

"I know Eira didn't, so don't play coy with me."

"I owe you a meal. We were going to have this the day of the cathedral."

"Good thing I don't have to work tomorrow." She took a sip. "That is strong!"

"You really are a lightweight, aren't you?"

"I told you I was. I was a studious student in college. All I ever wanted to do was save lives." She turned to her meal while Axel's heart skipped a beat.

That was how he felt.

That was all he'd ever wanted to do. He'd

focused so hard on school and walking the same path as his brother in hopes that his father would like him.

That he would make his father proud.

He realized that he and Betty were the same.

She took a bite of the lamb. "That's really good!"

"I'm glad you like it," he said, trying to find his voice.

"You know what, your father likes me, perhaps I can—"

He held up his hand to cut her off. "I don't want you getting involved with this."

"But you want to be a cardiothoracic surgeon. You have the skills, the knowledge, so you *should* be one. You should make your father listen."

"No, Betty. Don't."

"I won't, but you should do what you love, Axel. Life is too short."

He fell silent. That was so true. Life was too short.

He knew first-hand how short it could be.

They finished their meal, chatting about everyday things at the hospital. It was nice. Betty enjoyed every time they got together because it helped her to feel like herself again, to remember who she was before Thomas, before the loss of her father.

She was smiling and laughing a lot, but that was because of the beer she'd drunk. At least the hangikjöt had been served with potatoes so she definitely wasn't drinking on an empty stomach.

"Are you okay?" he asked, grinning, those blue eyes twinkling.

"Fine." She was a bit buzzed, but she knew what was going on.

"I'd better take you home." He paid the bill and they slipped out of the booth. And as they maneuvered through the crowds of people who were escaping the cold on a Friday night, his arm went around her. His strong hand against the small of her back as he guided her to the exit.

It was cold and crisper than it had been when she had left the hospital. She shivered.

"Are you cold?" he asked.

"A bit."

He slipped off his jacket and put it around her shoulders as she protested, because she didn't want him to freeze.

"I'm wearing a thick sweater and my car is just over there."

He put his arm back around her and guided

her to his SUV, which had been fixed from the
crash. As they walked, Betty looked up at the
sky and could see the faint green lights to the
north of the city.

"Oh! They're back out."

Axel craned his neck. "Yes. I heard they
were going to be particularly strong tonight."

"Too bad the city is drowning them out,"
she said.

"Would you like to see them better?" he
asked.

"Sure, but how?"

"I know a place. About an hour outside the
city. Eira is safe at her friend's house for the
night and you don't have work tomorrow. I can
take you, if you'd like?"

"Sure."

Even though she knew she shouldn't go on
a dark drive with him an hour outside the city,
she couldn't help but say yes. It was a once in
a lifetime chance to see the aurora borealis.
She had to take it.

Axel helped her into the SUV and then
climbed in the driver's side.

He drove away from the old town of Reykjavik and stopped at his place.

"I thought we were going to see the northern lights?" she asked.

"Yes, you stay put. I'm going to grab you a warmer jacket."

He was in and out of his house within minutes and was carrying not only a jacket, but an ugly knitted cap and a blanket.

"Here," he said, tossing her the pile of stuff he'd collected as he got back into his SUV.

"Thanks," she said dryly.

"Ready to see the aurora?"

"Ready."

He grinned and nodded. They drove out of Reykjavik north-west along the coast. Soon the lights of Reykjavik and then a few other small towns were behind them. The rest of the world was dark and restricted to the headlights of Axel's SUV and the other vehicles and trucks that were heading south toward Reykjavik.

After a while he pulled off in a lay-by, by the water, and parked. He turned off the lights and got out. Betty followed him.

It was dark and she could hear waves hitting the shore; she just couldn't see the water because there was no moon.

"I can't see them," Betty whispered.

"Why are you whispering?" Axel asked, whispering back.

"I don't know." She chuckled.

"Just be patient and let your eyes adjust. And you'll be rewarded. Just keep your eyes focused above you."

"Don't you mean north?"

"No, I can see the ribbon—it's above us. Iceland is above the sixtieth parallel, which means we can see them above us and extending across the sky to the north."

Betty closed her eyes and then opened them. As her eyes began to get used to the darkness she saw the first burst of color, in a green and purple ribbon, rippling and dancing across the sky.

"Oh!" she gasped.

"Aren't they something? I could watch them for hours."

"Me too," she whispered in awe. Tears stung her eyes at the beauty of the dancing lights in the darkened sky.

"You're crying?" Axel asked.

"It's kind of moving."

"I think it's sweet that you're crying."

"You do? Surgeons don't cry, though. That's what I was told by my father."

Axel touched her cheek, wiping a tear away with his thumb. "I think it shows more humanity when a surgeon cries."

Her heart was pounding like a jackhammer, her pulse thundering in her ears as she stared into his eyes, the aurora dancing above them. It was just the two of them in the cold darkness. Usually that would freak her out, but for some reason in this moment with his arms around her she felt safe.

She felt at peace.

She felt like herself.

And before she could react, Axel cupped her face and leaned in, kissing her. Tenderly at first, before it deepened. His mouth on hers, his hand cupping the back of her head as he kissed her with passion she'd never felt before.

It scared her, but thrilled her too.

"I'm sorry," he said breathlessly as he broke the kiss off.

"Don't be sorry," she said breathlessly. "Oh, the lights are gone."

He looked up. "Ah, that's the thing about auroras. You need a clear sky and there's clouds rolling in. Could be a storm. I think we'd better head back to Reykjavik."

"Good idea."

She wanted to talk more about what had happened just now. To tell him that it was okay that he had kissed her, that she didn't want things to be weird between them again.

That she wanted more than just a kiss under the Northern Lights, but her time here was limited and she had to find herself again before she got caught in another life that wasn't hers.

CHAPTER ELEVEN

IT WAS AT times like this that she wished she had someone to talk to.

After Axel had dropped her off on Friday night, she hadn't gotten a wink of sleep. Which was fine as she had Saturday off to try and catch up on rest, but instead she'd found herself sitting in her little cottage by the sea staring at the walls and going crazy. That was when she'd decided that she would just go to the hospital and do some administrative work or maybe convince the senior Dr. Sturlusson to let her do a surgery or two. Or at least have some of the more experienced residents do one while she watched.

One thing she knew, she couldn't just do nothing, because then all she would do was think about Axel's arms around her. The way his hands had felt in her hair, the taste of his lips and the way she'd absolutely melted.

And she had never melted like that for anyone before.

She walked over to the hospital and entered through the front doors, rather than the emergency-room entrance.

"Betty!"

She turned to see who was calling out to her and it was Stellan. She groaned inwardly. Stellan was handsome and charming. She'd gone out for coffee with him the day after he'd taken her back to Axel's place so she could watch Eira, but it had been the most tedious coffee she'd ever had. Stellan was a wonderful guy. But for someone else.

"Hi, Stellan," Betty said quickly.

"I didn't think you would be in today." He looked pleased to see her.

"Well, I'm not really here, but I thought I would get some work done anyways."

"I guess if you don't know many people it can be boring here."

"Yep, that's so true."

Stellan rubbed the back of his neck. "Look, if you're not busy later tonight I would love to take you out to dinner."

"That's very sweet, but I'm not here to date. I'm only here for three months to work with the surgical residents on this work exchange."

Stellan's cheeks flushed red and his jaw clenched. "I see. Well, I'm sorry."

"I would love to stay your friend. You're an amazing guy."

A small smile broke across his face. "I would like that too."

Then he stepped forward and pulled her into an embrace, before kissing her. It caught her off guard. She pushed him away.

"Stellan, I can't."

"It was worth a shot," he said with a shrug before leaving.

What was with *the men in Reykjavik?*

And as she tried to regain her composure she looked over at the stairs that led to the walkway that connected two parts of the hospital. Axel was standing on the walkway, leaning over the side watching her.

Crud.

She started walking toward him and he met her halfway down the stairs. His jaw was clenched and his expression unreadable. And Betty felt bad. She wasn't the kind of girl to kiss multiple men in a span of twenty-four hours.

"What did Stellan want?" Axel asked, crossing his arms.

"He asked me out."

Axel didn't say much.

"I said no," she said and she pushed past him and headed up to the walkway. She heard Axel following her.

"It didn't seem like you said no when he was kissing you."

"He initiated that kiss, not me and, honestly, what is it to you? We're not dating." She regretted the words as soon as she'd said them.

His eyes narrowed. "No, we're not exclusive. And no, we're not dating. I just kissed you in a moment of…"

"Weakness."

His expression softened. "What're you doing here today?"

"I'm going stir crazy in my cottage. So, I'm here to do paperwork and if I'm needed on a surgery then so be it."

Axel laughed. "You hope that you are."

"I am a surgeon. I'd rather be in the operating room."

"Well, I'll be sure to let you know if you're needed down in the emergency room."

"Thank you." She stopped in front of her office and opened the door. "Feel free to dump a couple of residents on my roster today. I can always get them to do labs on my post operatives. In fact, I think I'll do a round, so definitely send up a couple of residents."

Axel nodded. "I will. Though my father will be angry. He wants all the residents in the emergency room. The problem is they're tripping over each other down there."

"Do you want me to ask your father for residents?"

"No, I will send them." Axel lingered in her door as she took off her coat and set down her bag.

"Is there something else you wanted to talk about?" she asked.

Axel slipped into her office and shut the door. "It's not really something to ask. I want to try something out."

"Oh?"

And before she could answer, she was back in Axel's arms again and he was kissing her. And this kiss was night and day to the surprise kiss she'd received from Stellan. Stellan's kiss had been unwanted and she'd been detached.

Axel's kiss had caught her off guard, but it fired her blood. Her knees went weak and his mouth was hungry, hot over hers. He pulled her tight against him. His hands roamed down her back to her bottom and she couldn't help but let out a little moan.

He broke off the kiss and she had a hard time catching her breath. She looked up at him and his eyes were twinkling.

"What do you want to try out?" she asked breathlessly.

"That."

"Oh?"

"I wanted to make sure it wasn't just the Northern Lights or the beer affecting you."

Betty couldn't help but laugh and he laughed with her, his arms still around her.

"What's the verdict?" she asked.

"It wasn't just the Northern Lights," he said huskily and he kissed her again, a light kiss, but it still made her forget about everything.

"I'd better go," he said reluctantly as he stepped away from her. "Do you still want me to send those residents up?"

"Yeah," she said, trying to calm the erratic beat of her heart. "That would be great."

Axel chuckled and left her office, shutting the door behind him.

Betty leaned against the wall after he left and slid down to the floor.

More confused than ever, but also secretly pleased that it hadn't just been the beer or the romantic backdrop of the aurora borealis. Axel and she had chemistry, but if she didn't put a stop to this soon, she'd regret this.

She wasn't going to hurt Axel.

And she wasn't going to risk her heart. She'd done enough of that already.

Axel hadn't been able to get Betty out of his head all night. The way she tasted, the soft silkiness of her hair and how her body had fit perfectly against his. Just thinking about her body pressed against him made his blood heat.

He'd come to the hospital early because he couldn't sleep. All he'd done was think about Betty being in bed with him. Then he'd thought of her in the shower. She was everywhere, all at once.

And then he'd seen Stellan kissing her and the green-eyed monster of jealousy had reared its ugly head.

Mine.

That had been the single thought in his head when he'd seen Stellan kissing her. He was angry and even though he shouldn't care, because they hadn't promised each other anything, he couldn't help himself. He wanted Betty.

Even though he knew there was a time limit on their romance, he wanted to spend as much time as he could with her. He wanted to have this one, fleeting moment of pure joy in his life. Once she left to go back to New York, then he could return to normal.

Can you?

He shook that thought from his head.

Once he got to the emergency room he assigned two eager surgical residents to help with Betty's post-operative rounds and run labs.

And then he headed to check on Mr. Bjorn.

"Good morning," Axel said brightly as he entered the room. "How are you feeling this morning, Mr. Bjorn?"

"Sore," Mr. Bjorn said.

"Incision pain?" Axel asked.

"No, it's like before, but in my arm and it hurts when I breathe."

Axel snapped on gloves. "When did this pain start? Overnight?"

"No, just about half an hour ago."

Axel took the patient's blood pressure and it had dropped. It was hard to get a pulse in the arm that he was complaining hurt. He used his stethoscope to listen to the patient's labored breathing and one thought popped into his head. Mr. Bjorn had an embolus. It could be in his lungs or near the repair. It was hard to tell, but Axel knew that he had to find the clot soon.

"I'm going to do a CT angiogram. I think you might have a pulmonary embolism. So I need to find it and take care of it as soon as I can. I don't want anything to compromise your aortic repair."

"Okay. Will you be doing it, Dr. Sturlusson? I trust you."

Axel nodded. "Of course. I'm going to have some surgical residents prep you, while I prep the angiogram, okay?"

Mr. Bjorn nodded.

Axel left his room and called over Dr. Einnarsson, who had been in the original surgery. Dr. Einnarsson looked none too pleased to be beckoned by the black sheep of the hospital, but Axel didn't care.

"I need you to prep Mr. Bjorn for a CT angiogram. Then you can assist me as we look for a pulmonary embolus."

"Of course, Dr. Sturlusson."

Axel nodded and headed toward the angio suites, which were located at the other end of the hospital. On his way to the angiogram lab he ran into Betty, who had just sent her surgical residents off in the opposite direction.

She frowned when she saw him. "What's wrong?"

"Mr. Bjorn, our aortic dissection patient, probably has a pulmonary embolism. His blood pressure is down and his breathing is labored."

"Oh, no! That's horrible."

"I'm going to do a CT angiogram and, since I'm supposed to be on the trauma-room floor supervising the residents…"

"You don't need to ask twice. I'll man the trauma-room floor. You take care of your patient."

"Thank you, Betty."

They passed each other, heading in opposite directions, when Betty turned and called him back.

"What?" he asked across the causeway.

"What do I tell your father when he sees me working your shift?" It was asked in jest and it made him laugh. He needed a good laugh, because he was extremely concerned about his patient. He wasn't going to let Mr. Bjorn die because of a pulmonary embolism. Not after the man miraculously survived such an extensive and complicated aortic dissection repair.

"Tell him the truth."

Betty smiled and waved as she turned back

the way she was headed and Axel made his way to the angiogram room.

Mr. Bjorn's angiogram went well. Axel was able to correct the pulmonary embolism issue, but he was worried about putting Mr. Bjorn on blood thinners. Especially in light of the fact that Mr. Bjorn had had a repair of a major blood vessel. If he was on thinners and the repair leaked, it would be disastrous.

Axel was going to have to spend more time at the hospital to monitor the situation more closely, but he knew one thing was for sure: the clock had reset on Mr. Bjorn's eventual return to Sweden.

Axel headed back to the emergency room and the moment he stepped onto the floor it was a flurry of excitement.

His father was standing in the fray shouting orders and Axel could see some of the residents that weren't with patients in the triage area were packing up supplies.

"What's going on?" Axel asked, confused.

"Where were you?" his father snapped, spinning around to face him.

"I was doing an angiogram on my patient."

"We have cardiothoracic surgeons for that!"

"I am a cardiothoracic surgeon."

"Not in this hospital. In this hospital you're a trauma surgeon, or have you forgotten your place?"

Axel clenched his fist. "It was my patient. Besides, Dr. Jacinth was manning the emergency room for me."

"I know. She's supposed to be off, but I admire her spirit."

At least he admired something.

"What happened?" Axel asked, biting back the snarky response he'd been thinking.

"There was an accident in Kulusuk, Greenland. They need our assistance, so I'm sending a team over in a plane."

Axel's blood ran cold. He closed his eyes as he heard the sounds of the helicopter's engine giving out. The explosion, the heat of flames and the sting of ice-cold water as he was pushed by Calder out of the side into the unforgiving sea.

"Who's going?" Axel asked quietly, his stomach churning.

Please don't be Betty. Please don't be Betty.

"Dr. Jacinth and a couple of residents are getting ready to head to Keflavik to catch their flight."

"Tasiilaq is close to Kulusuk. Why don't they send help?"

"They don't have enough surgeons to send to Kulusuk. They are the ones who asked for help and so I'm sending a team. It's the right thing to do."

"Of course," Axel responded dryly. Then he saw Betty pulling on a hospital anorak and filling her kit. The thought of anything happening to her was too unbearable.

"Axel, are you even listening to me?" his father asked in exasperation.

"I'll man the emergency room now, Father. You accompany the team to the airport."

His father nodded. "Okay."

Axel turned away. He couldn't watch Betty leave.

He couldn't breathe thinking about her in the sky over the stormy waters of the north Atlantic. They were so unforgiving. So cruel. It had no mercy.

It showed him mercy, but not Calder.

He closed his eyes again, clenching his fingers into his palm until it stung and then he flexed them again, willing the screams of the wind, the waves, Calder's lifeless body out of his mind, but instead of Calder he saw Betty in the water.

And that terrified him to the core.

* * *

Betty tried to find Axel before they left for the airport. She hoped he wasn't worrying too much about the flight.

Why would he worry? He's not the one flying.

The emergency in Kulusuk had been minor, thankfully, but there was an earthquake just off the coast of Kulusuk and there had been a tsunami. So those that weren't injured in the quake had been injured in the surge of water and ice.

Everywhere in the small community that clung to an island just off the coast of Greenland was decimated.

The plane landed in the community of Tasiilaq and they boarded boats to cross the sound to the island of Kulusuk.

Other emergency teams had arrived and there was a small triage area set up at the highest point of the village. It was in that tent that Betty worked the hardest she ever had in her life, in conditions that she'd never worked in before.

She'd been so used to the cleanliness of state-of-the-art hospitals. She wasn't used to this kind of raw, ragged work.

Her body was pushed to the limits as she treated everyone she could. And when the last of the patients were seen to, she boarded a boat back to Taliisaq with her team and then back onto a plane to Iceland.

She was exhausted. They'd been working for over twenty-four hours.

She'd only stopped to grab a quick bite to eat and to drink coffee to help keep her warm.

The two surgical residents that had come with her were curled up in the seat of the private plane that the hospital had chartered for them. They were sleeping, but Betty couldn't sleep.

She'd done the most intense triaging she'd ever done in her life.

All without Thomas. It felt good to know what she was capable of all on her own.

To be free of him.

It felt good to be out there and helping people and to be on the front line like that. She understood why Axel had followed his older brother into the tactical navy and why he enjoyed being a surgeon in emergency situations.

And she couldn't help but wonder if he missed it.

Thinking about Axel triggered something else too. It made her think about the kiss in her office. The kiss under the Northern Lights had made her swoon, but that kiss in her office. When he took her in his arms and hungrily kissed her. That was something she'd never experienced before. Not with such heat and intensity.

Just thinking about it made her body come alive, her blood heat and her skin thrum with sexual desire. The kind she'd only read about in books. She'd always scoffed at the idea of being that aroused by a kiss.

Thomas had always complained about her kisses or their lovemaking. He'd never thought it was good enough, which was his first excuse for cheating on her with the woman he married. Apparently he'd had heat with her, but not Betty.

The plane landed smoothly and a van was waiting to take them and their gear back to the hospital.

She was exhausted now. As soon as she dropped her gear and did her report on what was done in Kulusuk, she was going to go home and have a shower and sleep. When she got to the hospital she was expecting to see Axel on duty, but he wasn't.

That's odd.

She did her quick report and then headed

home. When she got home, she had a shower and instead of going to bed, she got dressed and decided to head to Axel's place to check on him. Something was bothering him.

She wasn't sure what it was, but there was something wrong and she wanted to make sure that he was okay.

Betty called a cab and was across the town and standing in front of Axel's door in under thirty minutes. His SUV was in the laneway, so he was home, unless he was out walking somewhere.

Her pulse was thundering between her ears and she was suddenly very nervous as that rush of desire that she'd felt in the plane came flooding back.

She took a deep breath and knocked on the door.

Axel answered it. There were dark circles under his eyes, he hadn't shaved and he looked weary. As if he'd been up as long as she had been.

"Hi, you…" Her words were silenced as his arms went around her and his mouth found hers, kissing her as if his life depended on it.

She wrapped her arms around him, her hands in his hair, and she pressed her body against his, but no matter how close she got to him, it wasn't good enough. She wanted more.

He pulled her inside and they kissed for a few more minutes, her butt pressing into the corner of the small credenza he had in the foyer.

"Ow," she finally mumbled against his lips.

Axel broke the kiss and looked down. "I'm sorry, did I hurt you?"

"No, it's just the corner of this thing is digging into me."

Axel chuckled and lessened his grip on her. "I'm sorry I was so urgent there, but I've been sick with worry."

"You look tired," she said as he stepped away from her and ran his hand through his hair. "Were you up all night?"

"When you got on that plane… I lost my mind."

She touched his face. "I'm okay. Flying is safer than driving."

Axel snorted; it was apparent he'd heard that before. "I just couldn't think with you up in the sky and me down here… I don't fly, Betty. Not since the accident and I just couldn't bear the thought of something happening to you."

"I'm okay. We made it there and back."

"I know. I can see that, but…" He rushed

toward her and cupped her face in his hands. "I'm glad you're here."

She closed her eyes and he kissed her. Gently. Her body was thrumming with need.

"Axel," she whispered. "I'm not staying in Iceland. You know I have to go back to New York."

"I know," he said, his arms around her. "I can't promise you anything, Betty. My life is not my own. I have Eira and my work."

She nodded. "As long as we're clear about the terms."

"What are you saying?"

"Is Eira home?" Heat bloomed in her cheeks.

"No, she's at a friend's house," Axel said, his eyes dark and his gaze making her body quiver with need. "Are you sure about this?"

"No, I'm not. I... I was told I'm not very good at it, but for once I would just like to have a moment of living just a little."

Axel smiled and whispered softly against her ear. "Just a stolen moment?"

She nodded. "I want you to make love to me, Axel."

Betty had never asked a man to make love to her before. Before, it had always embarrassed her, but right here and now she wasn't embarrassed. She wasn't ashamed of the desire that

Axel stirred in her. She wanted him and she hoped that he wanted her just as badly.

That was all she needed to say and he scooped her up in his arms. She cried out and then laughed with him as he carried her once again.

"This is the first time I've been swept off my feet like this," she teased, kissing him.

"I carry you all the time," he said.

"I know, but this time it's different."

"It's not that different to me," he whispered.

A shiver of anticipation raced down her spine. Instead of carrying her into the room she'd occupied he carried her to the end of the hall. To his room, with the large bed that was covered with a warm, thick, down-filled duvet.

He set her down on the floor in front of him. Axel gazed at her, running his hands over her hair and then down her face.

"You are so beautiful," he said.

Her heart skipped a beat. She didn't know how to respond, so she didn't respond with words. She slipped her hands in his hair and brought him forward to kiss her again. To let him know how much she wanted him. How she wanted nothing between them.

She just wanted him.

"I want you, Betty. From the first moment I

saw you standing in the airport in those sexy boots."

She chuckled. "Sexy? I thought you said they were ridiculous?"

"Ridiculous to mask the sexy," he growled playfully, nipping her ear lobe while his hands cupped her bottom, squeezing.

"Well, I thought you were sexy too. As well as broody and…"

Axel silenced her with a kiss. She didn't want to talk any more really. She'd been dreaming about being in his arms since she'd first laid eyes on him. She'd denied her desire for so long. She'd never let herself feel anything since her heart was broken and she never lived in the moment and did something like this.

She never really lived.

Betty wanted him with a fire that burned through her. She wanted him to be buried deep inside her. She wanted him to help her forget her heartache and sorrow. To wash away her past, so she could rise like a phoenix from the ashes.

"I want you naked," he whispered huskily.

A shiver of delight ran down her spine and suddenly she was a bit shy. She'd never gotten naked in front of a man in a brightly lit room.

It had always been at night, in the dark. This was unplanned and spontaneous.

It was thrilling.

As if sensing her shyness Axel pulled his sweater off over his head, baring his chest. She ran her hands down over his bare chest and over his rock-hard abs. He sucked in a deep breath as she ran her hands down to the waist of his trousers, teasing just underneath. She could feel his erection as he thrust his hips against her.

"Betty," he whispered. "You're torturing me with your touch."

She slipped off her jacket and tossed it next to his sweater.

His gaze was fixed on her. His eyes dark, twinkling and mesmerizing.

It excited her that he was watching her.

"Now your shirt," he demanded.

She pulled it off and was glad she'd worn her black lace bra rather than the sports bra that she had been wearing under her scrubs. Next she kicked off her boots and then undid her jeans, slowly, his eyes fixated on hers. She shimmied out of her jeans and kicked them away.

She was exposed, but suddenly she didn't feel so shy any more.

This felt right and it had never felt this right before.

He reached out and touched her face. She closed her eyes and just let the feel of his strong hands on her take over her senses. Axel wanted her just as much as she wanted him. Her need to have him, her hunger for him was just as intense as his. She'd never felt that way before.

"God, Betty. I need you."

She moved away from him and sat down on the edge of his bed, sinking against the fluffy duvet. Axel undid his trousers and pulled off his underwear.

Heat flushed her cheeks. He came over to the bed and pressed her down against the mattress. His body over hers.

"So beautiful," he murmured again, stroking her cheek first and then trailing his hand down over her body, leaving a trail of gooseflesh in his wake. She arched her back, his touch making her burn with a need she'd never experienced before. A sense of excitement and pleasure that she wanted never to end.

Axel began kissing her, but not her mouth. His kisses started on her neck and went lower. Down over her breasts, to her stomach and even lower. She gasped when he pressed a kiss against her inner thigh.

"Relax," he whispered. He slipped off her underwear and her body shuddered in delight. When he kissed her thigh again, a rush of heat flushed her body and then when he kissed her, pressing his mouth to the center of her heat, she cried out.

Oh, God.

The pleasure that was rushing through her was sweet, but torture. She wanted him inside her. She wanted Axel to help her chase away the ghosts. To help her move forward. She didn't want to be haunted or hiding in the shadows any more.

She wanted to be freed.

"Betty, I want you. You're so wet, so warm," he said, his voice deep as he stroked her.

"I want you too. Do you have protection?" she asked.

"I do." He got up and pulled out a condom from his nightstand drawer. She took the package from him.

"What're you doing?" he asked.

"I want to help you." She opened it and rolled it over, touching him, stroking him. He closed his eyes and moaned.

"Betty," he murmured and he bent down, his hands in her hair as he pulled her up to kiss him. Their naked bodies flush, nothing between them now.

She pulled him down against her, opening her legs as he settled between her thighs, pressing his erection against her, one arm bracing to keep his weight off her, the other hand, stroking her and making her wet with need.

She thrust her hips against him, silently begging him to take her.

She wanted him. And she wanted him now.

He thrust forward, slowly sliding inside her. It had been so long since she'd felt this way. She rolled her hips, urging him to go faster. To take all of her. She was his. In this moment, there was no other.

She wanted him to go faster, but he held her hips, guiding her to meet every one of his controlled thrusts until she came, crying out. He quickened his pace then and it didn't take him long before he followed her. He collapsed on his back beside her. She rolled over on her side and he slipped his arm around her. Her legs were shaking, her body still quivering with heady pleasure.

His fingers made small circles on her upper arm.

The only sound was their breathing.

There were no words to say. Her eyes were

heavy…she was completely exhausted. So she didn't say anything. She wasn't even sure Axel wanted her to stay, but he didn't move and she was too tired, so she fell asleep in his arms.

Sleeping in a kind of warm safety she hadn't felt in a very long time.

CHAPTER TWELVE

AXEL WATCHED HER SLEEP. He'd been pacing all night before she'd arrived, the memory of his own accident at sea haunting him.

Calder haunting him.

When Betty showed up on his door step, it was all he could do not to take her right there. The whole time she was in Kulusuk he'd thought of her.

It was scary how much he thought of her.

How much he wanted her and how much she wanted him. He didn't deserve a woman like her. And their time was limited. She'd told him she couldn't stay in Iceland. She'd told him that she had to return to New York.

You knew this going in.

Except, he was falling for her. Completely.

You can't have her.

Look what happened with Freya. She couldn't handle it.

Betty is different.

Axel slipped his arm out from under her. She shivered in her sleep and he covered her with the duvet that had gotten twisted and kicked off the bed when they were making love.

He knew that the trauma team that went to Kulusuk had been working non-stop for over twenty-four hours. She had every right to be tired and he wasn't going to disturb her. He'd let her sleep, but he needed to make himself more presentable for when Eira came home.

Eira!

How was he going to explain this to Eira? She was almost fifteen, but he hadn't brought a woman home since Freya. And Calder had never dated again after his wife had passed away as he'd been too busy raising Eira.

If Betty woke up they could figure out what to tell Eira together. Eira loved Betty. She thought the world of her but he didn't want to get Eira's hopes up that Betty was staying, because Betty would be going back to America when her time was up here.

He quickly got dressed and then checked on Betty. She was still fast asleep. He slipped out of the room, shutting his door and headed downstairs, just as the front door opened.

"Uncle Axel?" Eira called out.

Axel held up his hand. "Betty is upstairs sleeping."

Eira grinned. "Oh, really?"

Axel crossed his arms. "She just got in from Kulusuk."

"Was she helping with the earthquake victims?" Eira asked as she set her bag down.

"She was."

"I want to ask her about that. My science project is all about earthquakes and tsunamis. I would like to get her opinion about the medical needs in the after…" Eira winced in pain as she tried to hang up her jacket.

"Are you okay?" Axel asked.

"Just woman's stuff." She winced again, her face pale. "It's been about a month, I suppose. I guess it's starting again."

"Do you want a heating pad?" Axel asked.

"Yeah." Eira was doubled over and a bunch of warning bells went off in Axel's head.

Eira sat down on the couch and Axel brought her a heating pad, plugging it in. Once she sat back she perked up, but he still wasn't convinced that it was normal pain.

"I'm sure that Betty would be happy to answer your questions when she gets up."

"Good," Eira said and she flicked on the television, keeping the volume down low. Axel left the living room and went back upstairs to check on Betty. She was sitting up in bed, holding the comforter to her chest.

"How long was I out?"

"Not long, maybe an hour. Did Eira wake you up?"

"I think so," Betty said wearily. "It's okay, I should get back to my place."

"I'll drive you back home, but Eira wants to talk to you."

Betty was pulling on her clothes. "Oh?"

"About her science project. She's doing a project on earthquakes and their aftermath. She learned you were in Kulusuk."

"I'd be happy to help her."

Betty finished getting dressed.

The silence between them was a bit awkward.

"So what happens now?" Betty asked, breaking the tension.

"We go on as normal. I have to stay in Iceland and you have to go back to New York. There are no strings."

"Good. Good. I hope we can still see each other while I'm here...as friends."

Axel smiled gently and touched her cheek. "I would like that."

I would like more, only he didn't say that

thought out loud. There could never be more with them. This was all he could ever have with Betty and he had to get used to the idea.

"What did you tell Eira when she learned I was here?"

He laughed softly. "I think she figured it out, but I told her you were sleeping because you'd been in Kulusuk. That's right before she doubled over in excruciating pain. She says it's her time of the month."

Betty's brow furrowed. "Excruciating pain?"

"She says it's been happening for a day or so. She's downstairs with a heating pad. Maybe you could take a look?"

"Of course."

They'd walked down a few steps when Axel heard the sound of someone retching and screaming in agony.

He was downstairs in a flash and found Eira in the fetal position on the floor.

Betty dropped down to face Eira. "Eira, sweetie, talk to me."

"It hurts," she cried.

"I know it does, sweetie, but you need to tell me how long this has been going on."

"A few days. Crampy pain, nausea."

Betty checked her radial pulse. "It's weak.

Call an ambulance. I think she has adnexal torsion."

Axel's stomach twisted. "She's too young for that. She just started her cycle."

"It happens during the onset. It's uncommon, but it does happen and I need to get her to the hospital to do an ultrasound."

Axel nodded and dialed emergency services.

Betty was trying to keep Eira calm, but Axel could tell that she was just as worried as he was feeling. The ambulance came and he opened the door for the paramedics. It was Stellan and his partner.

"Dr. Sturlusson," Stellan said and then Axel saw Stellan's eyes light up when his gaze landed on Betty. "Dr. Jacinth, what seems to be the trouble?"

"Acute, persistent abdominal pain in the lower left quadrant. Accompanied by nausea, a low systolic. I will ride with you in the ambulance. She's my patient."

Stellan nodded and Betty stepped back as Stellan and his partner got Eira on a gurney and then got an IV with a bolus of fluids and painkillers started on Betty's direction.

Betty climbed into the ambulance with Eira.

"I'll be there shortly," Axel said as he locked up.

Betty nodded. The ambulance doors shut and then took off. There were neighbors out, including Mrs. Ingborn. The woman had tears in her eyes.

Axel crossed the lane. "It's probably nothing, but she's got the best doctors watching her."

Mrs. Ingborn nodded. "Please keep us posted."

Axel nodded and then returned to his SUV. He started the car and went as fast as he could to the hospital. The ambulance had already arrived and he entered through the emergency-room doors to find his father pacing and shouting.

His father turned on him.

"Where were you when Eira came in with suspected adnexal torsion?"

Axel pushed past his father and found out what exam room she'd been taken to. His father followed him.

"How could you not see the signs?" his father shouted.

Axel spun around. "Be quiet!"

"What?"

"You heard me." Axel left his father standing there sputtering. It felt good to tell him off, even if it wasn't everything he wanted to say to him, but he didn't want to deal with his father's attitude. Not now when Eira was ill.

An adnexal torsion, or twisted ovary, was rare but it was serious. She'd been feeling crampy for days. Hopefully there was no necrotic tissue and if there was a growth in her ovary, which was a cause of a twisted ovary, it was benign.

Eira was only fourteen. She didn't deserve this.

And he couldn't help but think of Eira's mother who had died from an ovarian cancer only four months into a miraculous pregnancy. She'd refused to terminate and thankfully Eira was born safely. Soon after Magdalene had held her daughter for the first time, she had passed. The cancer had spread into her lungs.

Axel paced outside the exam-room doors, the curtains drawn to protect Eira's privacy as they did an exam.

Betty came out of the room, shutting the door behind her. Her expression was grim.

"It's adnexal torsion, isn't it?" Axel asked and he felt as if he might throw up.

"It is," Betty said grimly. "And there's a mass, but I won't know anything until I go in there. You're her guardian, can you sign the consent forms at the nursing station and I'll prep her for a laparoscopic surgery?"

Axel nodded. "Of course."

Betty slipped back into the room.

Axel couldn't think straight.

He just hoped the tumor was benign. He'd already lost Calder, he couldn't lose Calder's daughter too. He'd promised to take care of her.

Axel signed the forms and by the time he'd finished filling out all the paperwork, he was able to go into the exam room to be with Eira until they took her to surgery.

Betty had already left to prep for surgery.

He stood in the door. Tears were stinging his eyes as he stared at the last living connection that he had to his beloved late brother. She was so pale and wincing in pain in her sleep. They had sedated her to help with her anxiety and her pain.

Axel took a deep breath and sat down next to Eira's bed. He took her hand that didn't have the IV in it and held it.

He had a sense that someone was looking at them.

Axel looked up to see his father standing in the doorway.

Eira stirred. "Grandfather?"

His father didn't say anything.

"Grandfather, is that you?"

Still his father didn't respond and Axel watched in sadness and horror as his father turned away from his granddaughter's cries for comfort.

"I'm scared, Grandfather!"

"I'm here," Axel whispered gently. He climbed into bed beside his niece. She was still groggy from the medicine they'd given her. She clung to him.

"I'm scared, Uncle Axel. I don't want to die. Don't leave me."

"I'm here. I'll always be here."

Eira began to weep. "My father said the same to me, but he wasn't."

"I know, but I am here. I promise you. I'm here and you'll be fine."

Eira nodded and her crying slowed down. "I love you, Uncle Axel," she whispered before the medicine that she had been given to help her sleep did its job again. Axel laid her gently against the pillows, brushing her red curls off her forehead.

He wiped her tears gently. "I love you too, Eira. I'm sorry I'm not your father, but I love you and I will be here for you. Always."

"We're ready for her," Betty said from the doorway.

He was embarrassed to be caught crying over his niece.

He nodded. "Take care of her."

"I promise I will. As surgeons we're taught to tell the families of our patients that we can't promise much, but I promise you, Axel, that she will be fine. You have my word."

Axel crossed the room and kissed the top of her head. He wanted to pull Betty closer, but he didn't want her to have to change her scrubs.

"Thank you," he whispered.

She nodded and the porters came in to wheel Eira away.

Betty walked alongside them.

All Axel could do was stand in the hall and watch the last piece of his late brother be wheeled away. He felt so helpless.

Just as he had when his brother had died.

When his brother had slipped from his hands.

His heart was being torn in two and he was lost.

Completely lost and powerless, just like that day two years ago and he hated that. He hated this feeling. And once again he hated himself for surviving, because Calder would be stronger. Calder could have handled this and he wasn't sure that he could, but he didn't have a choice.

So he did what every person waiting for their loved ones did. He went to the waiting room and paced.

Hating to be on this side of the surgical-wing doors.

Betty was scrubbing her hands and going through the procedure. She'd done several adnexal torsions of the ovary. Usually by the time they came to her through the emergency room in New York there was necrotic tissue and she hadn't been able to save the ovary.

She was just hoping that with Eira it was caught early enough and that the mass she'd seen on the ultrasound was benign, because if it was malignant then she would have to perform an oophorectomy and then consult an oncologist about treatment.

Eira was too young.

Of course Eira's mother had been too young when she passed and although Betty didn't know what kind of cancer killed Eira's mother, she couldn't help but wonder if it was related to this. Eira looked so small under the draping on the surgical table.

Tears stung Betty's eyes and she swallowed the emotions that were threatening to overtake her so she could focus and save Eira's life.

You've got this.

When she closed her eyes she could see the broken expression on Axel's face as he'd watched his niece being wheeled away from him. The memory only strengthened her resolve to see Eira through this.

She finished her scrubbing and headed into the operating room, her scrub nurse helping her into a surgical gown and gloves. Dr. Einnarsson, the surgical resident, was waiting near a table with the laparoscopic equipment.

Betty felt as if someone was staring at her and she glanced up at the gallery to see Axel standing in the shadows. Their gazes locked and she nodded, letting him silently know that she had this.

Betty stepped up to the table.

"Eira Calderdóttir, aged fourteen, about to undergo an exploratory laparoscopic procedure because of suspected adnexal torsion. A mass was seen on the transvaginal ultrasound that was approximately four millimeters. Dr. Einarrsson, will you make the correct incisions for a laparoscopic procedure of the left ovary?"

Dr. Einarrsson nodded. "Yes, Dr. Jacinth. Scalpel."

She glanced back at Axel, who was watching Dr. Einarsson closely.

Once Dr. Einarsson was finished Betty was able to use the laparoscope to see the ovaries clearly.

Thank God.

There was no necrotic tissue, but the ovary was twisted and there was a small mass growing at the end.

Dr. Einarsson took over the camera portion of the laparoscope as Betty untwisted the ovary and then moved to excise the mass.

It was delicate work, but she was successful. Once she had safely packaged the mass she handed it to an intern.

"Take that to pathology. It's a rush. I need the results before I can proceed. I can't wait days. I need it now."

"Yes, Dr. Jacinth." The intern rushed out of the operating room. Now was the hard part of the surgery.

Waiting.

Was the mass benign or malignant?

Betty held up her arms so as to not contaminate them. She looked back at the gallery and Axel was leaning against the glass, his eyes closed and he was murmuring to himself. A lump formed in her throat and she tore her gaze away and looked back down at Eira, tape on her beautiful eyes to keep her eyelids shut.

So young.

It was a lifetime before the intern returned. "It's benign, Dr. Jacinth."

Betty closed her eyes, tears threatening to spill down her face, but she held it back and looked up to see Axel on his knees, his hands over his face, weeping.

"Well, let's repair the ovary and close her up," Betty said brightly.

Eira was going to live. She'd have to be watched and monitored in case this happened again, but the mass was benign. She didn't have cancer and for Betty that was the greatest news in the entire world.

Betty watched as they took Eira out of the operating room, and then peeled off her surgical gloves and mask. She sat down at a table with a computer and typed up her operative report.

Axel had left the gallery once the laparoscopes were removed and they were closing her up with paper sutures. He was probably on his way to the post-anesthesia care unit to sit with Eira. She would check on them both when she had done her operative report.

"Dr. Jacinth?"

Betty looked up to see Axel's father, Dr. Sturlusson, in the door between the scrub room and the operating room.

"Dr. Sturlusson, are you here to inquire about Eira?"

A strange expression crossed his face. "I suppose."

It was cold and Betty was taken aback by it. "The mass was benign and the ovary was saved. I did not have to perform an oophorectomy."

"Good." But Dr. Sturlusson's expression was blank and unreadable.

"That's not why you're here, is it?" Betty asked.

"No, there's a surgeon here from New York who has come to see you. Dr. Welling is waiting in your office."

Betty's stomach dropped to the soles of her shoes. "Dr. Welling?"

Dr. Sturlusson nodded. "He is the head of general and trauma at your hospital in New York, is he not?"

"Yes," Betty said dryly.

"Well, I told him you were in surgery and that you'd come as soon as it was over."

"Good," Betty said, but she didn't feel easy about this. Why had Thomas come? Why was he here? Why couldn't he just let her go?

Dr. Sturlusson nodded and left the room.

Betty finished her operative note and then pulled off her surgical gown and scrubbed out. She didn't take off her scrub cap as she left the surgical floor and headed up to her office. Where she really wanted to go was to the post-anesthesia care unit to check on Eira, but she had to get rid of Thomas first.

She didn't know what he was doing in Iceland, but he was not welcome.

Deep breath.

She opened the door to her office and shut it behind her. Thomas had been pacing and when he turned around, her heart skipped a beat, but instead of feeling that sense of euphoria and heartbreak she was used to, she just felt annoyance that he was here.

"Thomas, I'm surprised to see you here and, on that note, what *are* you doing here?"

Thomas smiled at her, the way he did that had always made her weak in the knees. "You're starting to sound like these people.

So straight and to the point. Aren't you happy to see me?"

"No," Betty said and she crossed her arms. "Aren't you supposed to be on your honeymoon?"

"I am, but there's been a problem at the hospital and I had to come home early and deal with it."

"I don't see you dealing with it as you're here standing in front of me," Betty said.

"Come on, Betty, don't be like that."

"What's going on, Thomas? I don't have time for this. I have a patient to check on in the post-anesthesia care unit."

"A high-profile patient that we've both worked on has come into the hospital and I need you. You're the best at laparoscopic surgery."

That was the first time he'd ever admitted it. She did excel when it came to laparoscopic surgery.

"Is it Jemima Whiting, the senator's little girl?" Betty asked.

"It is."

Jemima was a ten-year-old cancer survivor. She had colitis when she was seven and a J-pouch placed when part of the colon was removed. Jemima had survived stomach cancer and Betty had been there every step of the way. Jemima's first surgery had been the first time Betty had used a laparoscope.

Betty adored Jemima and her parents. It was Jemima's struggles that had formed the basis of Senator Whiting's platform and he continued to fight for free health care. When Jemima was hospitalized the press noticed. Betty was pretty sure that the press was probably camped outside the hospital now and since Betty was the best at laparoscopic surgery Thomas had come to get her. But he would take the credit, as always.

If it were any other patient, he wouldn't have come, but she'd bet that the senator asked for her personally.

"Okay, I will come over and perform her surgery, because it's Jemima, but once I'm done the surgery I need to return here and finish out my contract."

"Actually, Dr. Sturlusson released you from your contract."

"What?" Betty gasped.

"I told him that I needed you back to head up our new laparoscopic program at the hospital and the surgeon from Reykjavik wants to return. Dr. Sturlusson completely understood and knew that you couldn't pass up this opportunity."

The idea of heading up a laparoscopic program for surgical residents in New York was tempting, but Dr. Sturlusson and Thomas had no right to decide this for her.

What if she didn't want to go?

"What opportunity?"

Betty spun around to see Axel hovering in the door. She'd thought she'd shut the door when she'd come to confront Thomas, but she hadn't.

"Who are you?" Thomas asked rudely.

"Dr. Axel Sturlusson," Axel replied coldly. "And you are?"

"Dr. Thomas Welling. I'm Head of Trauma and General Surgery in New York at the hospital Betty works at."

Axel's gaze flicked to her briefly. "And you're leaving?"

"Yes, but—"

"Good luck to you, then," Axel snapped.

"Axel!" Betty went to leave, but Thomas held her back.

"Betty, we have to go. Our flight leaves soon."

"Let go of me!" She snatched her arm back and left her office, chasing after Axel. "Axel, wait!"

He turned around, his expression like stone. He didn't say anything to her as she approached him.

"I was going to tell you."

"That you're going back? You don't need to. I heard from Dr. Welling," he replied, his voice hard and cold.

"I'm going back to help a patient of mine and then I was planning to come back…"

"Until you were offered an opportunity you couldn't pass up. I get it. When Thomas comes calling you go running." He moved closer, his eyes dark. "You told me you were trying to get your life back on track, to step out of his shadow, but you're not doing that. He'll always have this hold on you."

It was as if she'd been slapped. Tears stung her eyes. She was going to tell him that his father had released her from her contract before she'd even accepted, but she doubted that Axel would believe her and she was so hurt by what he'd said.

"That's not true," she said, her voice shaking with anger and sadness.

She realized she had let herself fall in love again with another man who was going to hurt her.

"You should take the job in New York. The

head of a laparoscopic program is an amazing opportunity. I wish you well."

"You could come with me," she said.

"I have Eira. I can't leave."

"Because you're afraid to!" she snapped at him. "You let all this supposed baggage of Eira, of your PTSD, of your brother's death hold you back. The guilt of surviving when your brother didn't. Not all women think that's a burden. Not all women are like Freya."

"At least I have a legitimate excuse for letting something hold me back. What you're doing is pathetic."

Betty slapped him; it shocked her that she could be angry enough to strike him. She turned on her heel and left him behind without another word.

She should've known better than to let herself fall for another surgeon. To open up her heart and let someone in.

She was better off on her own.

CHAPTER THIRTEEN

HIS HEART HURT.

And he was regretting what he'd said to Betty, but when he'd seen Thomas and heard that she was being offered such an amazing position, he'd thought the kinder thing to do was to push her away. There was nothing here in Iceland he could offer her that measured up.

His life was not his to give. His heart, though it belonged to her, wasn't his to give either.

You're a coward.

He hung his head, trying not to let the storm of emotions raging inside him come out. He had to be strong for Eira, who was still sleeping and having a hard time coming out of the general anesthesia.

Axel reached out and took his niece's hand.

The best news he could've heard that whole surgery was that the mass growing on her ovary was benign. Once he knew that she was out of the operating room he'd gone to find Betty, to pour his heart out to her, but then he'd overheard the conversation between her and Thomas.

And he knew he had to let her go.

He had to push her away.

He couldn't hold her back.

"How is she?"

Axel looked up to see his father hovering in the doorway. He wasn't looking at him or Eira. Axel felt the rage that he had toward his father spilling over. His father couldn't even come in the room to check on his own granddaughter.

"The mass was benign," he said.

"I know. Dr. Jacinth told me," his father said.

"Aren't you the least bit relieved?" Axel demanded.

"How dare you insinuate that I don't care?"

"How dare I? How dare you?" Axel leapt to his feet. "You blame me for Calder's death, I get it. I blame myself, but you treat Eira with the same cold-hearted distance that you give me. You're a bastard."

His father's eyes widened in rage, but he couldn't formulate words.

"I'm sorry I lived, Father. I'm sorry your favorite died, but he died saving my life. How do you think that makes me feel? I loved Calder too." Axel's voice slipped. "He died and I am paying for his death. You're mad at him for dying, you're mad at Mother for dying, but I didn't kill them."

His father broke down then, weeping. "I am mad at them. I'm mad at them for leaving us. The three of us alone. How dare they do this?"

Axel's heart melted and he took his father into his arms and held him.

"I'm sorry, son," his father said. "I...the thought of losing you and Eira was too much for me to think of. I thought it would be easier to harden my heart. To push you both away, so that when you were taken from me, it wouldn't hurt so much. No parent should have to bury their child."

"It's okay. I know, but he died a hero. He died doing what he loved. I wished it had been me instead of Calder, but—"

"No!" his father said sharply. "Don't ever say that again. I am not sorry you lived, Axel. I'm sorry for holding you back, but it was my fear. My stupid fear of losing you. I thought keeping you safe under my thumb would be the answer. I was wrong. So wrong."

Axel felt as if a huge weight had been lifted off his shoulders. His father didn't hate him. His father was just as frightened as he was. His father was worried about losing both of them and in doing so he masked his fear with indifference. He pushed away those he cared about, because he was afraid of the pain.

Just as Axel had done with Betty. He'd pushed her away because he had been so afraid of losing her and in the process he had lost her.

She was leaving for New York and she wasn't coming back.

"Grandfather?" Eira asked groggily.

They both turned around to see Eira staring at them in confusion.

"Are you two hugging?" she asked.

Axel laughed and his father sat down next to Eira. "I'm so sorry, Eira. I'm sorry for being so distant when your father died. I loved him so much. I love you so much."

Eira began to weep. "I love you too."

His father leaned over and held her. "I was so afraid of losing you, Eira. Things will be better. I promise. It will be better for the three of us."

Eira clung to her grandfather. "I miss my father too. I miss him every day and I missed you too, Grandfather."

Axel touched her head. "I'm glad you're okay, Eira."

"What happened?" she asked as she let go of his father.

"You had a twisted ovary. And there was a mass," Axel said.

Eira paled. "Cancer?"

"No," Axel said. "It was benign. Dr. Jacinth repaired the ovary and you didn't lose it. You'll have to have yearly ultrasounds to make sure it doesn't happen again and be aware of symptoms, but there's no cancer and the mass is gone."

Eira sighed in relief. "Where is Betty?"

"She went back to New York," his father said.

"Why?" Eira asked, looking at him with annoyance.

"She got offered a job that she couldn't turn down," Axel said. "She had to go."

"You mean you pushed her away!" Eira snapped.

"Your uncle didn't push her away, Eira. I released her from her contract so she could take the opportunity in New York. She's a fine surgeon. I would keep her if I could. So if you want to blame someone, it's me."

Eira looked sad. "Uncle Axel, you need to go after her."

"What's going on?" his father asked.

"Nothing," Axel said.

"You love her," Eira said.

"I can't go to New York. I have you and—"

"I'm fine. Grandfather can take care of me and I'll be in the hospital for a couple of days. You need to face your fear and get on a plane and go win her back."

"Eira, I can't. What if—?"

Eira shook her head. "Uncle Axel, you can't live in fear and pushing someone away to save your heart isn't working. You love her. Be with her. I don't blame you for my father's death. You know that. My father was a hero. I loved him, but I love you too and you're sacrificing your life because you survived. Don't—my father wouldn't want it this way."

Tears streamed down his face. "You're smarter than your years, Eira."

She smiled at him. "I know."

His father nodded. "Go. Bring her back. If she wants to come back there's a place for her permanently, especially since I'll be losing you to Cardiothoracic."

Axel was frozen. He wasn't sure he could do it. He wasn't sure that he could get on a plane, but he had to try.

He had to win Betty's heart back.

No matter how scared he was.

* * *

The flight back to New York was long and though Thomas happily chatted away, the way he always used to chat to her, she just didn't care any more. She'd thought she was doing well in Reykjavik, but Dr. Sturlusson had released her from her contract without any hesitation and without asking her if that was what she wanted.

When they landed Thomas drove her to her apartment in Manhattan and helped her carry in her luggage. She didn't have a moment to rest before they were headed back to the hospital.

Outside there was a gaggle of press.

All of them waiting for updates on Jemima's condition.

"The senator requested you specifically," Thomas said. "But I know how much you hate the press so I will speak to them after the surgery."

"Fine," Betty said stonily.

She didn't care.

All she could think about was Axel and his hurtful words.

She'd thought he'd loved her too. She'd thought there was something there and she had honestly thought about giving up her life here in New York to be with Axel and Eira. To have a family again.

It had been so nice having people to care about and who cared for her well-being too. To laugh and not feel so alone. To have someone who had her back at work. Who valued her as a surgeon and as a woman.

She hadn't realized how lonely she really was until she'd spent time with Axel and Eira. Being here in New York again without them, her life felt empty, but Axel had pushed her away. She should've known better than to open up her heart to him.

She was a fool.

They pulled up at the back of the hospital where there was no press and she followed Thomas inside.

"Welcome back, Dr. Jacinth!" Nurse Rodriguez said from the nurses' station in the emergency room.

Betty smiled and waved at all these colleagues of hers who never used to speak to her. Colleagues who had pitied her a bit when Thomas had cheated on her and left her high and dry. Colleagues who knew what she had been through, but had chosen to say nothing and to let her suffer alone.

At least this time they weren't looking at her with pity.

"I'm going to change into my scrubs. What room is Jemima in?" she asked Thomas.

"She's in Thirty-two B. In the private ward on the general surgery floor."

Betty nodded. "Let her know I'll be there shortly."

"Of course. I will see you up there."

Betty slipped into the locker room and found a pair of spare scrubs and her collection of colorful scrub caps still in her locker. She picked up a turquoise one with snowflakes from the pile.

It reminded her of the snow and walking through Old Town with Axel. Of how happy she'd felt with him. How he'd made her feel like herself again.

How he'd made her feel free.

She tied her hair back and slipped on the scrub cap and then changed into her scrubs and headed up to the general-surgery floor. She held her head up high, instead of looking at the floor as she walked through the doors.

"Can I have Jemima Whiting's chart, please?" she asked the nurse behind the charge desk.

"Jemima Whiting is Dr. Welling's patient and he has the chart," the nurse said.

"Since when is Dr. Welling her surgeon? I have always been her surgeon."

The nurse looked uncomfortable. "Dr. Welling has removed you from her case. I'm sorry, Dr. Jacinth."

Betty smiled gently at the nurse. "It's not your fault. I'll retrieve the file myself."

It was time to put an end to Thomas's dependence on her, or rather it was time to end his hold on her.

She was the surgeon Senator and Mrs. Whiting had asked for.

She could handle the press.

She could make her own decisions about her career.

And she knew one thing: she didn't want to work at this hospital any more. She would find a job somewhere else, even if Reykjavik had fallen through because two men who thought they knew better had decided her life for her and she had let them.

No more. She was done.

This was her life and she was going to take control of it.

Thomas was in his office down the hall from the nurses' station and he was going over Jemima Whiting's chart with the hospital's press secretary.

"Dr. Welling, can I please have a moment of your time?"

Thomas looked up. "Sure. Barbara, you remember Dr. Jacinth?"

Barbara nodded. "How are you, Dr. Jacinth? How was Iceland?"

"Wonderful. If you'll excuse us, Barbara?"

Barbara nodded and left, shutting the door behind her.

"Barbara is getting the conference ready for after the surgery."

"The nurse said that I was removed from Jemima Whiting's chart. She said that you're the lead surgeon now."

"Well, you were in Iceland."

"Yet you came to get me. You begged me to come."

Thomas sighed. "Betty, let's not get into semantics about this."

"I'm not performing the surgery, am I? You're going to take over and take all the credit. Why was I brought here?"

"Fine," Thomas snapped. "You're better at laparoscopic surgery, especially on pediatric cancer survivors. Senator Whiting requested you. Jemima wouldn't even let me examine her. She likes you and I told the senator and his wife you were in Iceland, but they didn't care.

Once she's under anesthesia, it won't matter. I need you to convince them that you're doing the surgery."

Betty was shocked, but she shouldn't have been.

Thomas was using her again. As he always did. As she always let him.

"Oh, I'll tell them that I'm doing the surgery because I *am* doing the surgery."

"What?" Thomas asked, his voice rising.

"You heard me. I'm doing the surgery and you're not to step foot in my operating room. And if you do step into the operating room I will report your deceitful behavior to the board."

Thomas's face went red and his eyes narrowed. "You wouldn't dare."

"Wouldn't I? Try me, Thomas. We can do this the civilized way and you can keep your reputation at this hospital or I will get the patient involved in this. There's an awful lot of press downstairs."

Thomas said nothing and handed her the chart. "You've jeopardized the job as head of the laparoscopic program here. It was my idea, by the way, to give you that job!"

"I never accepted the job and I don't want it."

His mouth dropped open.

"Goodbye, Thomas." She left his office and shut the door. Not slamming it. And when the door was shut she started smiling.

Inside she was screaming, jumping for joy.

She was free of Thomas.

He had no hold on her.

This was her life. She was a damn fine surgeon and she was going to save Jemima

She headed down the hall toward Jemima's room with her head held high. She knocked on the door.

"Come in," Senator Whiting said.

Betty stepped in the room and Senator Whiting's expression lit up. As did Jemima's, who was jaundiced and breathing through a nose cannula. Betty's heart sank seeing her and she was glad she had come back for her favorite patient.

"Well, it's about damn time you showed up, Dr. Jacinth. I told that Dr. Welling he wasn't going to do the surgery and he'd better fetch you." The senator was teasing; she could hear the relief in his voice.

"Well, he did fetch me. And I'm here now." Betty opened her chart. "Have they prepped Jemima for surgery?"

"Yes. I was getting worried that I hadn't

seen you yet," Senator Whiting said. 'What were you doing in Iceland anyways?"

Finding myself. Freeing myself.

"I was working with the Reykjavik hospital and teaching their residents. I even got to work at the front lines of a disaster."

Senator Whiting was impressed. "Really? Was that the earthquake and tsunami that hit Greenland?"

"It was. I was there helping out."

Senator Whiting smiled at her. "Good for you. I always thought your talent was over-shadowed here. Are you going to go back to Reykjavik?"

"I don't know, but I do know one thing—I'm leaving here. Maybe I'll volunteer with Doctors Without Borders or something like that. Go somewhere I can be of the most help."

"Well, if we pull through this, you come and talk to me and I'll make sure your talents aren't wasted."

"Thank you, Senator Whiting." Betty turned to Jemima, who was beaming at her, though it looked as if she was in extreme pain. "Now, let's get you ready and see what's going on."

Betty was exhausted. She hadn't slept since... Well, she couldn't remember. The last couple of days had been a whirlwind. First had been the disaster in Kulusuk and then Eira's ovarian torsion followed by the flight back to New York and a long laparoscopic resection of the tumor that had been growing on Jemima Whiting's liver.

Thankfully, the cancer hadn't spread and the cancer that was on her liver had been different from the cancer that had been in her stomach.

Jemima would need chemotherapy again, but the child had gumption and would survive it. Jemima was a fighter and Betty had just given her her best chance.

Betty had delivered the good news to the press and now she was looking forward to going back to her home and figuring out what her next steps were.

She changed back into her street clothes and packed her scrub caps in her bag. She wasn't going to leave them behind this time. She also cleared out the rest of her personal belongings and left her lab coat and her scrubs from the hospital in the locker. She didn't need them any more.

When she left the locker room Mr. Crisp, the head of the board of directors, Thomas and Dr. Vero, the Chief of Surgery, were waiting for her.

"Dr. Jacinth, a word," Mr. Crisp said as he beckoned her over.

Betty's stomach sank, but only for a moment. Then she didn't care.

She wanted nothing to do with this hospital any more.

This was her past.

"How can I help you, gentlemen?"

"We wanted to congratulate you on a successful surgery, Dr. Jacinth," Dr. Vero said. "And we'd like to offer you the job of Head of Laparoscopic Surgery at this hospital."

Thomas looked sullen.

"That is a very generous offer, but I'm going to have to decline. And, Dr. Vero, I would like to tender my resignation. I was on sabbatical while I was in Reykjavik, but I won't be returning to this hospital after all."

Dr. Vero was stunned and Mr. Crisp's face was like thunder.

"Betty, don't be a fool," Thomas snapped.

She glared at him. "I'm not being a fool, Thomas. I would never try to trick a patient into thinking that the surgeon she requested was going to perform her surgery and have another surgeon perform it because that surgeon needed all the attention on himself. I've taken the back seat too long at this hospital."

"But we're offering you a position as Head of Laparoscopic Surgery. You wouldn't be in the back seat any more, Dr. Jacinth," Dr. Vero said.

"If I stayed here, I would. Thank you for the offer, but I'm going to have to decline. Good day, gentlemen."

She turned and left them all standing there. Her palms were sweating and her heart was racing. She couldn't believe that she'd done that.

That she'd stood up and taken charge.

She didn't know yet what she was going to do, but she didn't want to stay in New York. She hailed a cab and the driver took her to the end of her street. Her flat was the top of a sought-after brownstone in Manhattan and she would contact a real estate agent in the morning to put it on the market.

As she walked down the street, she noticed there was a tall man lingering outside the steps to her apartment.

Her heart skipped a beat and she stopped in her tracks. It couldn't be him. He would never come to New York, but as she slowly walked closer she could tell that it was indeed him. It wasn't her exhaustion that was making her hallucinate.

He had come to New York.

Axel?

As if he'd heard her thoughts he turned and looked at her. In his hand was a bouquet of flowers and he smiled at her, gently. He was dressed exactly the same way that he'd been dressed when he'd met her at the airport in Keflavik.

Only this time he didn't look so annoyed, or so put out as he'd been that first day.

"Betty, I'm glad that I had the right address. I thought this was your house and I didn't realize that there are many different apartments in this building. I couldn't get in. The street signs are impossible to figure out. So many numbers."

Betty smiled, trying not to laugh. Numbers were a lot easier than some of the long street names in Reykjavik.

"You've been waiting in the cold?" she asked.

He nodded. "This really isn't that cold though. It's like spring."

As if to directly contradict Axel's words, it began to snow.

"What're you doing here?" she asked, finally finding her voice and getting her head clear.

"I think it's obvious." He held out the flowers. "I'm sorry."

She didn't take the flowers. "Axel, you said some…wait, how did you get here?"

"I flew," he said nervously.

A lump formed in her throat. "You don't fly, though."

"I flew for you. I faced my demons for you and, guess what, I can't live without you, Betty. I don't want to live without you."

The words stunned her and she didn't know what to say.

"I pushed you away because I was afraid of losing you. I didn't want to burden you with my life. It broke me when Calder died. I blamed myself and I didn't think that I deserved happiness. So I hurt you. And I'm sorry. I love you."

"I… I love you too," she said, her voice shaking. "I came back to help a patient. That's all. I didn't come back for Thomas and I didn't come back for a job I didn't even want. I came back for a patient, but I was going to come back to you."

"I know. My father told me."

"You spoke with your father?"

Axel smiled and nodded. "Who do you think is with Eira now? Eira is the one who urged me to come here."

Tears slid down her face. "Eira's okay?"

Axel nodded. "She's doing well and she would like you to come home."

"Your father released me from my contract."

"He'd like you to know there's a job waiting for you. If you'll come back to Reykjavik and be a family with me and Eira."

"Are you asking me what I think you're asking me?"

"I want to marry you, Betty. Eira and I will move to New York if that's what it takes to be with you. To have you in our lives. Eira loves you and I love you. I love you more than I ever thought was humanly possible. I think I loved you the first moment that I saw you."

"Even in the inappropriate boots?" she teased.

He smiled gently at her. "Yes. Even then. Will you marry me?"

She answered him by kissing him. His arms went around her and he kissed her as the snow fell softly around them. Axel loved her, just as much as she loved him. They could be a family, her, Axel and Eira.

She wouldn't be lonely, drifting. She would be whole with him by her side.

"Is that a yes?" Axel asked as he broke off the kiss. He was grinning at her.

"Yes. It's a yes."

He smiled and laughed, scooping her up in his arms and spinning her around.

"Let's go home," Betty whispered.

"To Iceland?" he asked.

She nodded. "To Iceland, but there's something that we're going to have to do first before I move to Iceland."

He cocked an eyebrow. "What's that?"

"I'm going to have to get a better pair of boots!"

Axel laughed and kissed her again.

And she kissed him back.

She had finally found her happily ever after. She'd found her partner, her lover, her best friend.

She'd found her family.

EPILOGUE

One year later

"THIS WAS A FOOLISH idea and I don't want to be here."

"You can do it, Uncle Axel!"

Axel stood on the steps that led down into the geothermal waters of the blue lagoon and Betty stood next to him. He thought this was a silly idea, but Eira and Betty had outvoted him and told him it was a brilliant idea and he had to play along.

Eira was already in the water. It was Betty's plan to help him overcome his fear of water by easing him into the blue lagoon, so she was standing next to him, trying to coax him down the steps.

It had been slow, but he was getting there. And the blue lagoon was a calm, warm and relaxing environment.

"You got this," Betty whispered to him.

"If you say so," he muttered.

"Look, I'm not going to be the only one taking our kids to swimming lessons."

Axel grinned at her, his wife, who was just as feisty since that first day when he'd hoisted her over his shoulder at Keflavik Airport a year ago.

"I'm not too sure," Axel teased.

"I am. You conquered your fear of flying to come and get me and this water is warm and therapeutic." Betty took a step down into the heated pool. She teetered a bit and Axel reached out and steadied her.

"Betty, you've got to be careful. It's slippery and you're unbalanced."

"And whose fault is that?" she asked.

Axel grinned and reached down to touch her rounded belly. She was five months pregnant and just starting to show, but that didn't slow her down in the least. Sure, it made her more clumsy, but it didn't stop her from doing her work at the hospital, heading up a world-class laparoscopic program.

Nor did it stop her from helping him raise Eira, who was just as excited as they were about her new little cousin joining them in four months. His father was excited to have another grandchild and Betty and Axel had agreed that if it was a boy they were calling him Calder.

"Come on, Axel." Betty held out her hand. "Don't leave the mother of your unborn child hanging."

"Hanging?" Axel asked. "Is this another American colloquialism?"

"Yes. Take my hand."

Axel took her hand and slowly took the steps down into the warm water. His breathing steadied and he accepted that this was nothing like the ocean. This was warm and shallow and quite nice. He wrapped his arms around Betty.

"Yeah, Uncle Axel!" Eira hugged them both and then swam away to join a group of friends.

"Thank you," Axel whispered.

"For what? Marrying you? Having your baby? Getting you in the water?" She was teasing him.

"For everything. Yes, for being my wife, for being a strong woman for Eira to look up to, for being a fantastic surgeon and for making me whole again."

Betty stood on her tiptoes and kissed him on the chin.

"Ditto."

"What?"

"Ditto, it means I feel the exact same thing

about you. Thank you for helping me find myself again. For making me stronger. I love you." She kissed him again. "Now, let's go float around. I want to feel a little bit lighter, before I feel much heavier."

Axel reached down and touched her belly again. He smiled as their baby kicked and he could feel the little jab on his palm. His life was whole again.

He was finally healed.

He was finally complete.

* * * * *

If you enjoyed this story, check out these other great reads from Amy Ruttan

A Date with Dr. Moustakas
A Mommy for His Daughter
The Surgeon King's Secret Baby
Navy Doc on Her Christmas List

All available now!